"You've made two promises today, Brook Savage, and you can't keep them both—

You have to give up your vow to kill the Comanche, or cause me sorrow. I love you, Brook, but not enough to watch you waste your life and mine on senseless revenge."

He didn't look at her, but rode on ahead, his broad shoulders taut against the buckskins. She could read the anger in the set of his jaw, the ramrod-stiff tension of his spine.

Presently he dropped back and took a deep breath. "I can promise I won't go looking for Running Elk . . . but if he comes across my path—" Savage paused to see how she was going to take it— "I'll have to kill him. Something in me won't let him live after what he did to my family. I can't let that . . . atrocity . . . go unpunished."

MARYN LANGER is a popular writer of romance fiction. Her works include *Moon for A Candle*, *Wait for the Sun*, and *Divide the Joy*. Langer resides with her husband in Albion, Idaho.

Whispers on the Wind

Maryn Langer

Heartsong Presents

ISBN 1-55748-357-4

WHISPERS ON THE WIND

Edited by Anne Severance

PRINTED IN U.S.A.

one
1844

Brook Savage leaped from his chair and pushed his face within a nose length of Colonel Mallory's doughy profile. "You mean you won't send help to that wagon train, even when you know they're tracking straight for raiding Comanche?"

"You heard me right, Savage. You're paid to scout for the Army here at Fort Leavenworth, not ride out like a white knight to save every greenhorn who decides to break the rules." The colonel bent over a sheaf of papers on his desk, and Savage knew he had been dismissed.

Savage stormed out of the office in a rage. Mallory's penchant for military regulation and his total disregard for protecting human life continually infuriated Savage so that, out of spite, he frequently did all sorts of dumb things. For example, he knew better than to ride alone into the jaws of the Comanche, yet that was what he had to do, seeing as how he was the only hope of survival for yet another wayward wagon train. Furthermore, they probably would not believe they were in serious trouble and would consider his arrival an unwelcome intrusion into their affairs. These stubborn eastern know-it-alls were rarely grateful for help until it was too late and they were in the process of being scalped . . . or worse.

Nevertheless, he rode away from the fort on a May morning that showed every sign of being unseasonably harsher and hotter as the sun moved toward midday. With the sleeve of his buckskin blouse, he wiped at the trickles of

5

sweat running from under the dirty-tan plains hat and down the channels of his smooth-shaven face—a face that bore the faded deep scars of smallpox contracted when he was a child.

Savage turned west and let the smell of the land freshen his soul. Hock-high grass bent and shook, the tips taking on the look of shallow wind-driven waves, turning the prairie into a featureless sea of white sun in an endless blue sky and variegated green grasses rolling timelessly to where they met. This was his country, God's country. Though he had tried to leave it, settle down among his own kind, chain himself to kin and land and belongings, do the things expected of civilized men, he had failed.

Retreating to his childhood haunts in the heart of the Rockies to lick his wounds, he had found a woman who understood him. He had made her his wife, had built a home far from the edge of civilization and filled it with love and little ones. Then suddenly, five years ago, everything had been taken from him in a brutal senseless massacre. He had searched until he learned who had led the cowardly attack against a defenseless woman and two small children, and one day, when the time was right, Savage would even the score.

Until then, the only place he had found any comfort was here on the prairie, feeling the touch of the wind on his face, smelling the fragrance of tree and plant it carried down from the mountains, letting the land cry and grieve with him as it tried to draw the sorrow from his heart.

He rarely admitted the fact, but at forty he was lonely. Yet he could not leave the prairie and the Rocky Mountains. The best and essential parts of his soul were bound here. Bound by the work he did.

His thoughts drifted on the wind until, above the crest of a rise in the distance, a puff of smoke rose, quickly spread thin, and vanished. Savage tensed and his stomach knotted with dread. With the Comanche out raiding, there was no telling what he would find on the other side of that hill.

Making himself as small a target as possible, Savage bent over his horse and hung off to one side, Indian style, and rode toward the plume of dust. Before he reached the crest of the hill, he reined in his horse, slid from the saddle, strung his field glasses across his back, and crawled belly down up the grassy slope. The grass, lush and thick this time of year, hid him from any but the sharpest eye, and allowed him to take his time surveying the scene.

Well, there's that fool wagon train that's gotten itself off the trail and into trouble, he thought with some irritation as he looked down into a cluster of wagons tightly circled for the noon break. Lashed to the wagon tailgates, plows and fruit tree saplings with their roots bound in burlap protruded like large disfiguring growths. Water casks and crates of chickens clung precariously to shelves built along the sides of the wagons, destroying the original uncluttered design of the wagon boxes. These people were obviously farmers, carrying with them the basics for a new beginning, but if they were headed for Oregon, they were definitely going the wrong way! Ever since the Whitman party had made their way to Oregon country last year, there had been a steady stream of people eager to join them, but most of those groups had had the good sense to stay farther north along the Platte. Whatever had possessed these people to travel down into Comanche territory?

The dust cloud that had attracted his attention was made by a couple of scouts sent out from the wagons. Watching them ride toward him now with so little skill, Savage doubted they would be able to recognize an Indian were they to see one.

Before riding into the camp, Savage trained his glasses on the surrounding countryside. He could see no signs of Indians, but that meant nothing. The few islands of trees and dense brush that dotted this rolling sea of dark green grass could hide a raiding party from even the most knowledgeable.

Slowly he scanned the domestic scene below. The women were working together, cooking and cleaning up, while the men tended to the needs of the teams and hauled water. The older children gathered buffalo chips for the fires and watched over the younger ones. It seemed like a well-run group—no squabbling, each person busy with some task. Inside the circle of wagons, a group of men was making repairs on a wheel. Except for the fact that there was no lookout posted, he would believe they had purposely left the established trail and knew where they were headed.

Feeling he had seen enough, he was ready to lower the glasses and drop them back into the case, when a halo of ivory-colored hair braided into a coronet swept across his field of vision. He paused and watched the tall, smiling woman. Graceful as lakeshore reeds bending in a gentle breeze, she stood at the tailgate of her wagon, mixing and administering concoctions to the line of people passing by. Her face, serene and loving as she listened to each person's complaints, reminded him of a medicine woman he had known in the Cheyenne tribe. Once, she stopped to tuck several stray tendrils of white-blond hair up out of her way, and glanced in his direction. He nearly dropped the glasses. She had enormous eyes, blue as cornflowers, fringed with honey-colored lashes. Though he was sure she had not seen him hidden behind the hillock, he stared into the clear azure of her wide eyes and felt a strange sense of disembodiment.

He imagined her voice, soft and low, as she crooned to quiet the restless babies thrust into her arms, and a yearning welled in him to hear her voice speaking to him, soft and close. *Savage, you're one big idiot. You're an Army scout and your job is to find out where these people are going and report back to the fort. You do not need this woman or any woman to complicate your life again.* But his lecture failed to help. The longer he watched, the more he wanted to meet her.

He rode slowly, out in the open, his hands visible at all times. The last thing he wanted to do was take nervous greenhorns by surprise. When he finally arrived at the circle, she had finished her work and was standing some distance away from the wagons, alone in an island of cottonwood and sycamore trees, calmly observing his arrival.

There was a peaceful repose about her face that he had seen only on Indian women, and unconsciously he turned to ride toward her.

"Halt!" commanded a strong voice.

Startled, Savage whirled to see a short, heavy-set man with a battered Hall carbine aimed, ready to fire at him. He had underestimated these people. There *was* a guard, he just had not been obvious.

"Who are you and what are you doin' ridin' into our camp?" growled the well-muscled, red-faced guard.

The man seemed not the least intimidated by Savage, who was himself a big man, standing well over six feet, with a lean, hard body. Broad shoulders and thick muscular arms, developed from years of hard work in the outdoors, pulled the soft tanned buckskin shirt taut. But there was not the slightest tremor in the hand holding the gun or in the voice, and Savage knew he had better talk fast.

Slowly, he raised his hand and held it out to the side, away from his holstered pistol. "Name's Savage, Brook Savage, and I scout for the Army out of Fort Leavenworth."

"Ain't you got better sense than to ride in to a camp unannounced?" The guard's light blue eyes glinted with the desire to teach Savage that lesson.

Savage had formed a theory over the years—light blue eyes, though faded in color, were invariably sharp of sight and the man behind them, an expert marksman. "Mind if I swing down off my horse?" he asked, keeping his voice even and low. The man was already stirred up enough. He needed only a little more incentive to shoot.

"Yes, I mind. Up there, if you try to run for it, I can shoot the horse out from under you and still have you left for fun." He grinned as if daring Savage to enliven a boring day.

Light blue eyes also signified a short temper, Savage recalled, and he did not plan to provoke the bull-necked defender of the camp. "Mister," Savage began, "I just want to talk with your wagon master. He around?"

Flinty eyes remained locked on Savage, assessing his real business with the train. At last, the guard bellowed over his shoulder, "Enoch!"

"Be right there," called a voice from inside the circled wagons.

"Got us a stupid mountain man wants to talk to you," the guard said to a short, thick-waisted man scrambling his way over a wagon tongue and through the gear, stacked ready to load.

His hat pulled low to shade his eyes, Enoch hurried toward the waiting men. The horse, spooked by the approaching stranger, pranced a nervous side-hop, and Savage concentrated on quieting him, paying the rotund man little mind.

When he got around so he could see, Enoch broke into a wide smile of recognition. "Savage, you miserable cuss!" he exclaimed. "Get down off that there horse and let's have a look at you." He removed the battered felt hat and scratched at his mop of long curly white hair while he surveyed the scout.

Savage swung easily out of the saddle and clapped the wagon master on the shoulder. "Enoch Fisher!" he bawled. "Never expected to see you leading a train again."

"Never expected to, neither." Turning to the guard, the man's face a twist of bewilderment, his gun still trained doggedly on Savage, Enoch reassured him. "It's all right, Barth. This here's Brook Savage, scout from Fort Leavenworth, about fifty miles north of here on the Santa Fe Trail."

Reluctantly, Barth lowered the gun and, grumbling to himself, stalked out into the prairie.

His broad, florid face still beaming with delight at meeting up with his long-time friend, Enoch took Savage by the arm. "Come on over to the fire, you woodsy ol' critter. Let's get you some victuals and you can rest a spell."

Savage dropped the reins, an act his gelding Smoke took to mean "eat," and followed Fisher over to a dying fire. "Enoch, you old coyote, you're fifty-five if you're a day. Why haven't you given up traipsing over this lonely old prairie by now?"

Enoch chuckled and handed Savage a cup of coffee. "Said I would after that last trip, did not I? Savage, you know me—a sucker for a sad story. These folks was all ready to leave Independence when their wagon master up and disappeared on 'em. They was determined to come, with or without guidin'. Got themselves started right enough, but like most folks headstrong enough to tackle this country, they wanted to think for themselves and took a wrong turn. Heard this was a faster, easier route. When I learned from some drifters they'd seen this train travelin' straight into Comanche country—" He shrugged and looked a bit foolish. "Like I said, I'm a sucker for a sad story. Be on my conscience if I did not try to undo the damage before something serious happened to 'em." He paused and looked out over the prairie, heat waves distorting the distance, and rubbed the back of his neck. "I can feel them savages out there. Neck itches all the time and I can't smell a thing but Indian. Can't see 'em, though. You see anything?"

Savage shook his head and accepted the plate heaped with crisp fried potatoes and hominy grits. "I get the same crawling feeling you do, but so far I haven't seen signs of Comanche through this area."

Enoch snorted. "Huh! They're hereabout though. I'll be real glad when I can persuade these folks to head north and travel the proven trail to Oregon."

"Oregon! That really where they're headed?"

"So they say, but they're determined to make their own way. Hard-headed a bunch as I ever dealt with."

Savage shook his head in disbelief and began to eat quickly, aware that Enoch was eager to break camp. "I'm on my way back to the fort," Savage said and handed his plate to Enoch. "See what I can do about getting you an escort until you get up onto the Oregon Trail. Cheyenne country's a lot safer."

"For you, I reckon, boy. You're one of 'em. Not likely to be real healthy for the hair of this bunch though. Be much obliged for any help," Enoch said as he tossed the tin plate into the steaming pot of water sitting just off the fire. Then he acknowledged a summons with a wave of his hand. "Pastor Waite's callin' me. Or I should say that sister-in-law of his is. Gives me a right good idee for why she's a widow at such an early age. Bossiest woman I ever had the misfortune to travel with!" He cast a disgusted look in her direction and turned to leave. "Make yourself to home, Savage. I'll try to get back for a quick visit."

"Mr. Fisher, if you *please,* sir," the widow Waite called in an over-sweet voice, the kind that made Savage's skin crawl. "Your help is required here . . . at once!"

"See what I mean," Enoch said and rolled his eyes. "If you'll excuse me, we'll soon be ready to pull out."

Savage nodded and watched Enoch hurry over to where a short, red-headed woman was giving instructions on how to hitch up a team. The tall, stoop-shouldered man ignored her instructions, all the while arguing that this was not woman's work. Savage smiled and gave thanks that he was not mixed up with the likes of her.

Alone now, he was free to search out the golden-haired woman. Perhaps even talk with her. He looked to where he had last seen her, sheltered and well-concealed in the woods some distance from the camp.

With the sun dappling her faded calico dress, he almost missed her as she stood braiding her hair. Their eyes met and something in her look struck a chord deep inside, silent for years. Savage came alive with the warmth. A force outside himself propelled him toward her, and she took a step in his direction, their eyes still clinging. He felt the pulse beat in his temples and his mouth dry up. Suddenly, he grew shy and he felt a flush redden his neck and creep up into his cheeks. He had forgotten how to talk to a white woman. What would he say? *Howdy ma'am, you're one fine-looking lady.* He smiled at the sound of the ridiculous words in his mind, and she smiled a slow gentle smile in return.

Quickly, he removed his hat and dropped his eyes, lest she read too much he was unable to hide. It was then he saw her feet encased in soft beaded moccasins.

"Savage!" Enoch's gravelly old voice hollered. "We need those big ugly muscles of yours over here."

Like a shock wave, the old man's command ripped through Savage. In a way he was grateful. He was not dealing well with the emotions surging through him, and this was the perfect excuse to back away. He could not resist one final look, however, at the gentle, golden beauty, her fingers caught in half-finished braids. Without a word between them, she had stirred a fire in his blood such as he had not experienced for a very long time.

two

Esther finished braiding her hair, never taking her eyes from
the man Enoch had called "Savage." She knew, with a kind
of inner knowing, that he had been about to come to the copse
to talk to her when the wagon master unwittingly intervened.
Now she would have to wait to see if the tall scout would try
again when he finished helping with the wagon repair.

In the heat, the men, all except Pastor Waite, stripped to the
waist to heft the Cranney wagon and slide on the new wheel.
Savage shucked his dusty buckskin shirt, revealing his chest,
broad and smooth, coppery-tan in the sunlight. The great
muscles of his back and arms stood out like ropes under the
silky skin.

Excepting for Barth, Savage, with his tremendous
strength, put the efforts of the other men to shame, and
helped to make quick work of the wagon repairs. Then,
gathering up their shirts, the sweaty men loped to the stream
to wash. Esther could hear their wild splashings and wondered if they had undressed and gone swimming with the
children. She would not have blamed them.

Esther knew Savage would come, so while she waited, she
withdrew deeper into the thicket to a spot where she could
rest her back against a pecan tree. Here they would have
more privacy. He seemed the sort who, if he had an audience,
would do little more than acknowledge a woman with a nod.
She intended to make it easy for him.

She felt Savage's presence before the snap of a small stick
alerted her, and she jerked her head around to see him

standing a few feet away, arms folded across his chest, leaning against the trunk of a nearby cottonwood tree. His untrimmed shoulder-length hair was still damp and curled around his face as he stood motionless, eyeing her intently.

Now that he had finally come, Esther sat, unable to speak, clumsy with fear at the prospect of meeting the first man, white or Indian, for whom she had ever had any stirring of romantic interest. Though she looked in his direction, she could not bring any words of welcome to her stiff lips. Under his steady gaze, she grew embarrassed over the frenzied pattern her heart insisted on beating, and spread her hand over her throat to hide the pulse throbbing there.

She pressed herself back against the tree as though to retreat from his imposing presence. Why had she thought seeing Savage, speaking with him at close range, would be a good idea? She prayed to dissolve into the ground, away from those penetrating gray eyes.

That petition denied, Esther sat stiff as a board, nervously smoothing out the un-ironed skirt of her freshly washed dress, then cupped her hands in her lap as Sister Waite had taught her. Looking down, she stared at the bottom of his fringed leggings and his great feet, shod in moccasins. They were cuffed with a minimum of red and white beadwork along the edge. Dust clung to them, turning the pale leather a gray color and dulling the beadwork on top of the moccasins.

Savage did not move from the spot where he first stopped, but remained motionless, as if sensing that any movement would send her into flight. Finally, he cleared his throat softly. "I began to wonder if I would ever get close enough to talk with you." He spoke in quiet words, letting his voice flow to her. "Ever since I first saw you through the field glasses before I rode in, I have wanted to meet you."

His voice, deep and soft like the low rumble of distant summer thunder, fell like music on her ears and helped relieve her fears.

He cleared his throat and spoke again, even more softly, "I mean you no harm. Please do not be afraid of me."

He spoke to her as one would a skittish colt, and something in the tone of his voice soothed Esther, relaxed her taut muscles, invited trust. Gradually her heartbeat slowed, and the quivering began to subside.

His was a strange voice—rough, raspy, different from any she had ever heard—but it fit him. Esther found herself listening intently, all her senses alert. It was then she realized how gentle his voice was, understood with a rush of insight that it was filled with a kindness and caring foreign to her. To her surprise, Esther raised her eyes and found herself saying, "Please, come and sit."

Slowly, Savage walked toward her, his moccasined feet making no sound, and with practiced ease, he crossed his legs and, in one flowing motion, lowered himself to the ground in front of her. He sat, not speaking, as though waiting for Esther to begin.

Even under Sister Waite's expert tutelage, Esther had never been able to master the art of small talk. She thought it silly to toss her curls and say, "I do declare, sir, you say the nicest things," when a man paid a compliment. Besides, such superficial chit-chat seemed absurd to use with this wild stranger sitting at her feet.

The silence stretched, like rawhide being pulled to make a bowstring, and every nerve in Esther's body grew taut enough to pluck. Maybe she could mention how warm it was for May, she thought. Yes, that is what she would say. She cleared her throat, a tiny click of sounds, moistened her lips, and drew in a deep breath.

"My name is Brook Savage," he said, relieving her of the responsibility of speaking first. "Folks mostly call me Savage." He chuckled softly, deep in his throat. "They say it fits everything about me."

Relief spread through Esther, and the breath she held came out as a sigh. He was the most gentle savage she had known, but still she hesitated. She had learned through painful experience that the less people knew about her, the better off she was, the safer from hurt. If they knew nothing, they had no weapons with which to wound her. Now, to her amazement, she calmly introduced herself. "Esther is my name. Esther Wheeler."

Though Brook Savage's face remained immobile and closed, his eyes filled with a warm glow. "Pleased to meet you, Esther Wheeler." The strange voice dropped to a raspy whisper, "Mighty pleased to meet you."

Esther had not yet looked fully at the man called Brook Savage. It was not the Indian way. Even now, she found she slipped into those habits whenever she was faced with unfamiliar circumstances. Still, she longed to inspect Savage's features at close range, and this desire tugged at her like a magnet. Slowly she lifted her gaze to his face and watched the harsh mantle of the army scout fall from him. His face altered until a gentleness, a tenderness appeared in place of the hard unfeeling crust. The years seemed to drop away, the deep lines softened, and Savage smiled, warm and friendly. His eyes, filled with understanding and sincerity, shone like gray satin.

Esther found herself smiling back at him, burying her insecurities and self-doubts, withholding nothing, warming to him as she had to no other. "You deliberately snapped that twig, did not you?" she said at last.

He smiled again. "I had to do something to get your attention."

She returned a quick grin and watched the corners of his eyes gather into tiny folds.

They continued to sit in silence, a comfortable silence. This was how Indian men courted, Esther knew, the couple getting in tune with each other through the senses. White people talked all the time, their words often getting in the way of their true feelings. This was better.

But, as the minutes passed, she began to grow uneasy under the intensity of his gaze. She raised a small, tanned hand and plucked nervously at the wisps of hair curling at the nape of her neck.

Apparently sensing her discomfort, again he broke the silence, and in his rumbling voice, commented softly, "You're wearing moccasins."

Esther looked down at her feet, crossed daintily at the ankles. "I have for years." She paused, trying to decide if she should say more. After all, they had only just met. But the tilt of his head, as if to catch her every word, invited her confidence. "When I was returned from the Senecas by the good pastor and the widow Waite, I was expected to give up all Indian ways," she plunged in. "They purchased fine boots for me, but my feet cried with pain when I forced them into those stiff, heavy shoes. I could not keep my balance on the fashionable high heels." She shook her head sadly. "Poor Sister Waite finally gave up and let me wear the moccasins." Esther shook her head and a sadness crept into her voice. "Though I do try to do what she wants and be like the other white women, I do not often please Sister Waite. She makes it plain that she considers me her cross to bear in this life."

Not knowing what to do with her hands, Esther smoothed her wrinkled cotton skirt and waited for him to speak.

He chuckled softly. "Martyrs are hard to live with." Then, as if eager to set her at ease, he changed the subject. "How long were you with the Senecas?"

She tensed. A flush rose up from her neck and spread to color her face. The loathsome term "squaw woman" slipped into her thoughts, but surely Savage, who seemed so Indian himself, would not be thinking it.

Regaining her confidence under his look of acceptance, Esther decided to tell him her story in a condensed version. "A little over ten years," she began, barely above a whisper. "They captured me from the Delaware who took me when I was six." She bowed her head. Plucking nervously at the grass, she snapped it off and rolled it into balls between her thumb and forefinger. A deep frown furrowed her normally clear brow.

"Esther," he said tenderly, "I am aware of the humiliation you must have suffered at the hands of so-called Christian women because of your being an Indian hostage. I understand your circumstances completely and find no fault in you." Savage leaned forward, his expression of approval unchanged. "Tell me about your capture," he encouraged in a gentle rumble. There was no condemnation, no cold withdrawal. Though he did not yet know that she had never been forced into marriage or ill-used in any way, his words of unquestioning acceptance fell like rain on her parched soul, making it possible at last to talk of those years.

Looking into Savage's sympathetic face, she began. "The spring I was six years old, my family, the Daniel Wheelers, moved from Shenandoah Valley, Virginia, and settled on the

Blue River in Indiana.

"One afternoon when we had been there about three months and the men were away helping a neighbor build his winter cabin, the women and children arranged a berrying expedition downriver. When our baskets were full, we children, under the watchful eye of my Aunt Mercy, began a game of hide-and-seek. I chose a hiding place inside a deep hollow at the root of a great tree. That was a sad mistake. A gigantic bear already occupied the hollow.

"Nothing to this day has ever frightened me as much as when that great growling creature rose up out of the ground and lumbered toward me. I froze with the terror of it until the screams of Aunt Mercy, telling me to run, finally penetrated. I fled headlong into the dark tangled forest, paying no heed to where I ran. There were times when I could feel that bear's hot breath on my neck. For a time, I thought I had escaped, but by then, I was thoroughly lost.

"My next clear recollection is of waking up in an Indian lodge. Because I somehow had learned the language, I understood that I had been rescued by a group of warriors returning from a hunting expedition, camped for the night in a cave near where I fled from the bear. The men heard my screams and took me home with them. One had recently lost a daughter, and he took me to his lodge as a replacement for her.

"These people were very good to me, and I lived happily with them until the spotted sickness struck our village, and my Indian family became ill and died. After that, I was taken in by another tribe, and through a series of trades and sales, I became the slave of a Seneca medicine woman when I was twelve. She was also a white hostage who had spent most of her life with the tribe. She had a Bible and taught me to read and write and when we were alone, we spoke English. I served her and learned from her." Esther paused, thinking of those days. "Six months before I was ransomed, I was made her official assistant.

"Then the soldiers came to free me. Since it would require such a long time to locate my white family, if indeed they were even still alive, I was taken to a mission home. Because Pastor Waite was experienced in dealing with newly found hostages, they placed me with him. When he learned I was a healer, he permitted me to assist him. He also found for me the latest books on medicine and allowed me time to study. I took everything in the medical books that fit the way I believed. Now I practice my own brand of medicine, combining the best of everything I have learned . . ." she paused, measuring Savage with her eyes, "and submitting it, with much prayer, to the Great Healer."

Silence filled the thicket when she finished, and Savage reached out and took her hand, holding it gently in his large work-calloused palm. With the physical contact, her heart again jumped skittishly, and Esther dropped her eyes as a blush burned hot on her cheeks.

Savage gazed at her with unabashed admiration. "From the hill yonder before I rode in, I watched you through the field glasses as you ministered to the needs of these people. They came willingly to you with their medical problems. They trust you. That is a wonderful gift."

Bestowing a gratified smile for his compliment, she said, "I've done all the talking so far. I would very much like to know about you. You are also wearing moccasins, and you tread with Indian steps, noiseless and swift. Does that mean that, like me, you have spent much time with the People?"

He nodded and pursed his mouth. "Mine is also a long

story—" He cast an eye at the wagons, the teams hitched, and hesitated— "But there is not time to tell it. I think the train is ready to roll. I promised Enoch I would ride back to Fort Leavenworth and bring a military escort to see your group through to the Missouri River and onto the Oregon Trail. I will make certain I am part of that escort. We will have plenty of time then to talk."

"I understand," she said simply. "I will wait to hear more of your time with the Indians."

In the manner of nobility, he lifted her hand and kissed her fingertips, then held the hand and rose effortlessly to tower above her. With his assistance, she stood before him, the crown of her head coming just under his chin. Their eyes searched, locked, making silent promises.

"Enoch says Abigail Cranney's birthing time is soon," Savage managed. "Says, though the rest of the train will move on, the Cranneys are planning to stay put until she has her baby."

"Yes, that is their request. Abigail is in a very weakened condition. She may not survive even then. If there is no danger, perhaps they can stay even a few days more so she can have a bit more time to recover before being jounced in that wagon again." Esther heard a calm unemotional stranger talking and scarcely recognized herself. Such cool impersonal tones could not possibly be coming from her, not with the turmoil raging inside.

"Are you going to attend her?"

"The Cranneys do not look kindly on my kind of medicine nor on my background. I will stay with her only if I am asked."

He nodded. "I'll be back tomorrow afternoon with the troops. Whether you're with the Cranneys or with the train,

I'll come for you. Watch for me." His eyes begged for her promise.

She smiled. "I will watch."

Looking down into her face, he said softly, "If I'm not here by afternoon, do not give up. I'll come . . . no matter what."

Quite unexpectedly, tears of happiness pricked the backs of her eyelids and she turned away. Together, they walked from the copse to where his horse, having eaten his fill, stood hipshot, waiting.

"Tomorrow," he whispered as he urged her face around to look at him. Seeing the tears, he ran trembling fingers over her cheeks and wiped them away. "I'll come. Nothing will keep me from coming back to you. Nothing!" Then, he turned his back, stepped easily into the saddle, and rode away without looking at her again.

Through her tears, Esther watched until he rode to the top of the small hill. He reined up, turned and, silhouetted against the horizon, waved to her. Then, spurring the prancing gelding, Savage galloped out of sight over the ridge. Small puffs of dust drifted to the horizon to remind her in which direction he rode.

Standing there, suddenly bereft, she wondered if he was aware of the extra weight he carried away with him. For, in their brief encounter, she had given him her heart.

three

Running Elk, wearing only a breechclout and moccasins, rested in the brilliant afternoon sun. Rested for the first time in days and let his mind drift.

He was a handsome man with features that seemed chiseled from fine-grained mahogany and polished to a satin luster. Yellow paint ran in carefully applied streaks on his forehead, across his high cheekbones, down over a firm jawline, making him look fierce enough to frighten the most stout of heart. Still, though ringed with black paint, his deep-set dark eyes continued to reflect wisdom and generosity, traits that made men trust and willingly follow him on raids year after year. His silver-threaded black braids, wrapped in soft strips of beaver fur, hung long and thick over his shoulders. Though solidly built like his brothers, he was unusually tall for a Comanche and equally graceful on the ground or on horseback.

Running Elk carried few tokens of his coup, yet the People knew he always gathered more than any man in the raiding party. At twenty-one, he had been the youngest member of the Kaitsenko, the Society of Ten, the Kiowa's highest honor. Now, at thirty-three, he was their most honored war chief.

They had just completed the first foray of the summer season and again Running Elk, as their war chief, led them. The raids had been a great success, and the warriors had much plunder to take their women. Now they rested in the grove of tangled underbrush and cottonwoods by the river and divided the goods among themselves.

Running Elk, from his vantage point above the camp, looked out on the grassy softness just beneath the crest of a low hill. Looked north at the sun-drenched prairie unrolling before him. There was no sharpness in the landscape, no abrupt bluffs to break its flatness, no rocks heaved up to make a jagged skyline. The land flowed and curved and way off to the north, the cloudless sky curved and flowed to meet the greening land, soft and rounded like a woman.

He had been gone too long from his land, hard and bold, full of strength. Though the mountains were solitary, there was a majestic lack of symmetry in their ruggedness that relieved the eye. With each journey up or down the craggy peaks, there was a new path, a hidden magic to be discovered, ever changing, ever new.

Here in this place, the timeless, unceasing prairie wind, carrying with it the sadness of the long-reaching silent land, blew through his soul, leaving behind it the grieving feeling of something lost forever.

With apprehension, he studied the islands of trees and bushes dotting the plains, and suddenly he felt restless, uneasy. The wind seemed to talk through the trees, moaning with the voices of lost souls. The thick bushes growing under the trees were the friends of the enemy, giving them too many places to hide. A cold chill ran through him, and he shivered.

Turning his back on the undulating sea of grass before him, Running Elk shook off his melancholy musings and gazed down to where the men of the three Comanche tribes were busy changing the surcingles that held the packs and transferring them to fresh ponies. He sized up the large herd of stolen horses grazing along the slow-flowing river that snaked across the prairie. The People would make good trades with such fine animals.

When the chiefs of the other two tribes finished dividing their share of the spoils and climbed the hill to join Running Elk, one of them motioned to him.

"Do you see the dust cloud in the distance?" Tall Lance asked, folding his long thin legs under himself and dropping to the ground.

"I have been watching it," Running Elk answered. "When the wind blows right, it will clear the dust and then, with these 'magic eyes,' I can see everything." He held up the field glasses he had taken from the body of a Texas Ranger last week and handed them to Tall Lance.

Tall Lance examined the two metal tubes bound together in the middle. The ends were blocked with thick glass. He rubbed curious fingers over the slick surface and licked his lips in anticipation as he placed the two rings against his eyes. He moved the glasses up to the sky and down across the prairie, then over to the dust cloud with the wagon train underneath. All the while he looked, he kept up an excited running commentary on what he saw. "If only the dust would clear. I want to see more of the train of wagons. Will you let me look again?" he asked Running Elk.

Upon being assured that he could look through the magic eyes when the train became visible, he relinquished them to Ugly Owl.

Ugly Owl gripped them in his pudgy hands, turned noticeably pale, hesitated, then squared his fleshy shoulders, and set the glasses to his eyes. "Oh!" he gasped and lost himself in exploration.

"Running Elk, my brother," Tall Lance began, "I hope these white people keep coming west so we can raid them often. They bring such wonderful things, and they are easy to plunder—soft like newborn pups." Tall Lance, from the

Staked Plains Comanches east of Santa Fe, glanced again in the direction of the slow-moving line of wagons. "My people do not see things like this. With such riches for the taking, I may spend more time here in the east." He caressed the fine new rifle he had taken.

Ugly Owl handed the field glasses back to Running Elk and reached into the fringed bag slung over his shoulder. "I agree with our brother, Tall Lance. See what I have." He pulled out a small round mirror and, with his fingertips, explored the back decorated with intricately intertwined flowers and leaves etched in the silver. Turning the mirror over, he stared for a long time at his reflection, then handed the mirror to Running Elk.

Cautiously he took it, running his finger lightly over the cool, smooth surface of the glass. On occasion Running Elk had seen his reflection in still pools, but the image had been indistinct, broken by slight movements of the water. Now his large luminous eyes with their heavy fringe of black lashes stared back at him, unblinking in their intensity. The clarity of the reflection made Running Elk feel detached, as though he were outside of his body, observing his face from a distance.

"The one who made this has medicine, powerful medicine," Running Elk said, with a slight tremor in his voice. Handing back the mirror, he stared at Tall Lance's gun and continued in a faraway voice, "You are wrong, Tall Lance. The white people are not soft. A soft person could not make the new firestick you now carry. Always, with each raid we learn to our sorrow that they have new and better weapons. The white eyes are like the wind, never still, always changing." He held up the field glasses. "The people who make these things are not soft or stupid—" He paused and his eyes narrowed as he looked into the distance. "Unlearned about a new land, but not stupid."

"You talk as though you are afraid," Tall Lance taunted.

Running Elk stared hard at the wagon train. "I only wonder what the White Eyes you call pups will be like when they grow into wolves." He turned and his gaze pierced Tall Lance. "And never, never believe for one moment that they will fail to learn as they grow."

Again placing the field glasses to his eyes, Running Elk followed the slow progress of the wagon train. After a time he said in a voice almost too soft to hear, "Then we shall see who is the victim and who is the prey." Though the sun was four hours in the sky and already hot, he shivered again and slowly lowered the glasses onto the grass-carpeted ground.

"Do you want to raid the wagon train?" Running Elk asked the other two chiefs.

"Since you saw the train of wagons first, Running Elk, it is yours if you want," Ugly Owl said in a generous gesture of friendship.

"I agree," Tall Lance said. "We have been lucky so far and have much goods. My brothers are getting anxious for the warm beds of their women. There is no need to get greedy and make them weep when we do not return."

"I thank my brothers for their generosity. I accept the wagon train." Running Elk held out his hand and clasped the wrist of each war chief.

"We will continue to rest here until evening when it is dark and cool, then we will ride like the wind toward home," Ugly Owl said. "If we are favored, we will be home in two, maybe three sleeps."

Tall Lance nodded and, like young boys, he and Ugly Owl loped down the hill to tell the men of their decision.

Running Elk lay without moving a muscle. He propped his elbows on the soft earth and looked again through the glasses at the dust cloud. Just then, the late afternoon breeze came up and blew the dust away, revealing a long line of swaying white tops. Through the glasses he could see the women and children walking beside the wagons. Some of the men drove the teams, while others rode ahead as scouts. Even with the glasses, all these things looked no bigger than bugs. He would wait until they grew larger before calling Tall Lance for another look.

There was nothing new or different about this train to set it apart from all the others he had watched and raided. Today, however, he did not feel the urge to raid. He laid the glasses down and rested his head on the cool grass. He and his men would also stay here during the day and tonight continue their homeward ride north under the moon. The sun was still high enough in the sky to warm his back and make him drowsy. With no reason not to, Running Elk slept.

The train created its own music as it moved, a cacophony of wheels creaking on the hard ground, white tops flapping in the constant wind, harnesses squeaking, and the plodding teams grunting and wheezing with the strain. There was an uneven rhythm that soothed the civilized ear. To Running Elk, however, the sound and rhythm grated along his back, and he woke with teeth clenched.

Signaling to Tall Lance to hurry, Running Elk grabbed the glasses and looked down the slope in front of him at the passing caravan.

Tall Lance arrived panting, crawling at an incredible pace on his stomach so his silhouette would not be seen from below. Silently, Running Elk handed over the glasses and

Tall Lance accepted them, his hands trembling with eager-ness. He swept the glasses swiftly along the length of the train, murmuring his discoveries to Running Elk.

"I see a woman with nearly white hair braided high on her head, but she is young and beautiful. She walks proud, solitary, like a chieftain's daughter. You will like to watch her, my friend."

"Why will I like watching her more than you?" Running Elk asked, feeling a bit irritated that Tall Lance should think to choose a woman for him.

"My tepee is full and warm. Two wives take care of my needs. Besides, I like roundness in my women. This one is too skinny. It is you who need a woman to take care of you. This one is tall and slim. You like that kind, I have noticed." Just then Tall Lance paused, slid the glasses backward, and held the position. "Ah," he breathed, "here is one for me. Her hair is the color of new copper and it shines in the sun like fire. She is not very tall, and she is round in the right places." He took the glasses from his eyes and handed them to Running Elk. "Here, see the golden one for yourself. She walks near the front."

Slowly, Running Elk moved the glasses up and down the line of wagons. It delighted him how clearly he could see even the smallest detail. He watched the children playing tag, and the mothers hurrying them along when they fell too far behind. *How little difference there is between my people and the white eyes*, he thought. *And yet, we will not stop warring until one of us has won and driven out the other.*

He found the golden-haired one beside the first wagon walking alone as Tall Lance had described. Much as Run-ning Elk was loathe to admit it, Tall Lance was right. She did take his eye, and he held the glasses steadily on her. She walked with long graceful strides, the kind that ate up the miles without tiring the body. Unlike the other women, she wore no protective bonnet, and the sun shone full on her clear tanned skin. Her gold-white hair was bound in two thick braids wrapped high on her head and it shone like a halo. She wore the usual calico dress, but when he looked at her feet, he saw she walked in moccasins. His heart stopped. She was fair as a spring day, not a drop of Indian blood. What did the wearing of moccasins mean?

"Ah, you found the golden-haired one. I can tell," Tall Lance crowed, his wide mouth pulled into as much of a smile as the long scar across his cheek allowed. "She is a fine one. But look for the red-haired one near the back of the wagons."

Dutifully, Running Elk swept his lenses to the back. It was easy to spot the one who caught Tall Lance's attention. She was nothing to look at, short and dumpy, and she never stopped talking for a minute, even when the dust caught in her throat and choked her. *Foolish woman!* he thought disdainfully. Her throat would turn raw and bleed in another day or two if she did not stop coughing and drink little sips of water instead. Running Elk conceded that her hair was striking, but nothing else about her appealed to him. "If you want her, we will raid and take her," he told Tall Lance.

Tall Lance shook his head, reached for the glasses again, and followed the woman a bit longer. "No, I shall only dream of her," he said as he handed back the glasses. "My other wives would make her life one great misery if I brought her back. I would get no enjoyment from her." He looked at the train with sad eyes, sighed over the lost dream, then walked slowly back down the rise to the river.

Running Elk fastened the glasses again on the tall woman

and watched intently. Studying her as she walked, he learned much about her. No children flocked around her, and while the other women chattered like magpies, no one spoke to her. Nor did she speak. Once, she put up a hand to shield her eyes from the sun and looked directly at him. He knew she could not see him, but looking into her eyes gave him a strange feeling. On her hand, she wore no gold band that showed that a white woman was pledged to one man. Running Elk did not understand why. From what he could see, she was without flaw.

At that moment, a gaunt, raw-boned man rode up and talked briefly with her, then urged his horse on along the line of wagons. And once again she walked alone.

As though in answer to Running Elk's wishes, she stopped just below the rise where he lay and stretched as though reaching for sunbeams to put in her pocket. A brisk west wind picked up her skirt and billowed it out. Her elegant hands caught it gracefully and straightened the folds in place.

Running Elk could not get his fill of looking at her and followed her with the glasses until the train passed by and out of sight behind a hill on the horizon. When she disappeared and he knew he would not see her again, an icy void filled the place where his heart beat.

Closing his eyes, Running Elk remembered long ago when he returned to his camp from a hunt. At the memory, the stench of burning flesh still filled his nostrils. His skin crawled at the silence smothering the village, and he saw his heart's joy lying in front of his lodge, her soft white deerskin dress covered with dried blotches of blood.

Though he had attempted to appease his grief by wreaking equal acts of pain and devastation on the white man, hate grew inside him, dried his tears, and filled his heart. Her memory still brought the bitter metallic taste of hatred to his mouth, and Running Elk had, until this moment, looked without pleasure on other women, preferring to remember his beautiful bride.

Today, however, this tall, golden woman touched him, made him warm inside again. Perhaps it was time.

four

Darkness fell and the breeze died away. Mosquitoes whined around Esther's face as she felt her way out from the circle of wagons and along a tentative path, worn to the bank of the slow-moving stream. With the thick darkness between the last of twilight and the rise of a full moon, a hush settled over the land. Even the fretful cries of the children, exhausted from long hours of walking in the hot sun, quieted, and the murmured conversation of the men around the brightly burning fire ceased for the moment. Only an occasional cricket chirp punctured the stillness as though the little creatures were testing the air for the proper moment to begin their nightly concert.

Esther sank onto the grass-carpeted ground. It had been a long day for her, too, a day full of promise, and she was not ready for sleep. She craved, instead, a few minutes of solitude to savor her time with Savage before she had her evening prayers and returned to the wagons circled and chained tightly together. Besides giving fortlike protection for the people, the circled train provided an enclosure for the stock, beyond the easy reach of prowling Indians.

Because Abigail Cranney was in such pain with her impending delivery, the train had stopped early. A large tent had been pitched in the center of the wagon circle, a tent Esther had not been allowed near so far. A bent old woman threw back the flap and stepped outside. The firelight picked up the snowy white of her hair, highlighting the fluffy crown as she bobbed her way across the circle and out between the wagons into the darkness, while another woman with the vitality of youth, took her place.

A few yards from the tent, the fire burned bright and hot, and the scattered forms of blanket-wrapped children, bedded for the night, lay close around to gather warmth from the blaze. All the men, save one, hunkered down around it, visiting quietly. Out of reach of the flickering light, in the shadows behind the tent, a young giant of a man paced. This was Abigail and Joseph Cranney's first child and Joseph, in the tradition of the white people, was forbidden to be with his wife during the birthing, or even to know how things were going with her. As he paced, he nervously raked thick fingers through a mane of shaggy brown hair.

Esther wished she dared speak a few words of comfort and explanation to him, but she might as well be a leper, she thought, so repugnant was she to the others. Though they did not speak of it, she knew that the other women considered her soiled because of her Indian captivity, and seemed to draw back almost visibly whenever she came near. Consequently, she spoke to no one unless spoken to. Only with Pastor Waite did she feel remotely comfortable, and they talked only occasionally of mission work to be accomplished in Oregon when they joined the Whitmans.

One reason she had been so eager to travel across the uncharted continent was the hope that, in the West, she could leave behind forever the taint of her Indian life and be accepted for herself. Here among the women of the wagon train, however, Sister Waite had quickly spread the word of Esther's past, and any hope of her belonging had been rudely dashed. Though all but the Cranney family came regularly to Esther for cures for sickness, everyone remained cold and aloof, choosing to ignore her except as manners dictated.

Another scream pierced the air, split the silence, then left an echo wafting off across the plain. Esther clenched her hands and knelt to pray. *Dear Lord, please bring about some way that I can help Abigail in her time of need.* Esther paused and wondered if she should mention Savage. But her heart was too full not to. *And thank you for sending Savage, she prayed. It seems as though You prepared him to understand me, to accept me just as I am . . . the way You do. But even if he never becomes more than a friend, I will feel richly blessed.*

Esther stopped and pursed her lips. This next part of her nightly prayer was always difficult. *Lord, please soften my heart toward Sister Waite. She judges me so harshly when she knows so little about me.* Again Esther paused and a deep sigh escaped.

Another agonizing scream, this time more piercing and lingering, shattered the night. Those by the fire jumped up, and the children on the ground threw back their covers and leaped, trembling, to their feet. Women, wiping their hands on their aprons, came running from all the wagons and clustered around outside the opening of the tent.

Still another wrenching scream hard on the heels of the last brought Esther to her feet. Would they ever let her go to Abigail?

Joseph pounded up to the tent entrance just as Delia Cranney threw back the flap and stepped out, her eyes great dark holes in a white face. "I do not know what to do," she cried, wringing her hands.

The children cowered together, and the men and women looked at each other in helpless frustration until Joseph whirled and searched out Pastor Waite. After a quick conversation, Pastor Waite nodded. "Esther!" his voice boomed.

"Sister Cranney needs your help."

Esther gave quick thanks. She had prayed all afternoon that she could be of service. The women assisting Abigail had only borne babies. They knew nothing about delivering them. But from the age of twenty-one, she had been recognized as a healer by the tribe with whom she lived, the Seneca. It was a rare gift, she knew, bestowed by God on very few. Even after her return to the white man's world she had not taken the sacred gift lightly, nor did she ever refuse to use it when called upon.

"I'm coming," she answered, not looking forward to her reception at the birthing tent.

As Esther stopped by her own wagon to pick up her chest of supplies, Enoch Fisher stepped out of the flickering shadows near the lead wagon and fell into step beside her. "See if you can do somethin' about Miss Abigail's unbridled screaming. I realize birthin' ain't easy, but this moon ain't called a Comanche moon for nothin'. They cotton to raidin' at night under a full moon. I can't see no Indians, but I can smell 'em everywhere."

Esther nodded and hurried on. Arriving at the tent and kneeling beside the birth pallet, she placed her hand on the young woman's swollen belly. "Abigail, listen to me," she said quietly, "if there is an Indian within a hundred miles, he can hear you. This early in the birthing, please try to exercise some restraint and not bring down all the Comanche tribes in the territory on us. You'll have plenty to yell about later on."

Abigail opened her eyes and shot Esther a venomous look, but she pressed her lips together and tried to smother the next scream. Despite her efforts, however, the cry forced itself out as the contraction intensified. A low moan built in her throat, rising higher and becoming louder behind her clenched teeth, until she could contain it no longer. It burst from Abigail's lips in a shrill, dissonant shriek.

As the scream died away, Widow Waite slipped through the doorway, unannounced. "I know a bit about these things. You're going to need some help, Esther."

Esther looked up into the clear green eyes and wondered what on earth had possessed Jasmine Waite to volunteer to work with her. Sister Waite, as she liked to be called, rarely spoke directly to Esther, unless it became necessary to correct her manners or speech and thus civilize her. Even though Sister Waite had taken her into the home she made for Pastor Waite, had taught her how to dress, and trained her in proper manners and housekeeping skills, she had never treated Esther like an equal, had never discussed anything of a personal nature with her. Maybe now things would be different—

"I would be most grateful for some assistance," Esther said, trying to conceal her surprise at the offer.

Then she understood. It was not Esther the woman wanted to help. It was just that this event was the most interesting at the moment, and Sister Waite had to be a part of it, even if it meant sharing close quarters with someone she disliked.

Without further words, Sister Waite knelt, took the rag Esther had just used, and dipped it into the water basin. Wringing it out, she wiped Abigail's face with the cool cloth. In the light of the lamp, Sister Waite's hair, carefully parted in the middle and dressed into two thick coils in back, burned a hot copper as she bent over Abigail.

The contractions were still coming a considerable distance apart, and with Jasmine doing the only thing that could be done at the moment, Esther took the opportunity to rest and gather her energy for later. She sat back on the pallet and watched Sister Waite attacking the chore assigned her with the dedication and thoroughness with which she tackled everything, but with no joy.

Though round in shape, Jasmine's pinched face, the petulant set of her mouth, her green eyes darting everywhere into other people's business, coupled with a bossy manner, made her almost as friendless as Esther. But if Jasmine Waite were aware of the people's opinion of her, she never let on. Talking nonstop, she pushed herself into conversations, gave advice by the bucketload, and lamented loudly when it was not followed. She ran from morning to night, up and down the train, "doing her Christian duty," as she called it.

Esther often wondered how Pastor Waite endured his sister-in-law, particularly when it was she who was responsible for his losing pastorate after pastorate. As far as she knew, the only one he had ever left willingly was the ministry on the streets of New York when he decided to travel to Oregon.

Through the hours of Abigail's deepening labor, Esther continued to study Jasmine carefully, determined to find something praiseworthy about the woman. Then Jasmine lowered her head to peer more closely at Abigail, and the lamplight turned her hair to a burnished russet. Naturally curly, Sister Waite's hair was the most beautiful in the company, to Esther's way of thinking. If one looked at her hair and did not listen to her incessant drone, Jasmine was quite striking, so Esther concentrated all her attention there.

A moan as Abigail's contraction deepened, and Esther forgot the Widow Waite. "I am boiling some herbs for you to drink, Abigail," she explained. "It will help ease your pain."

Abigail's mother, Veraleen, gave Esther a studied look. "You delivered any babies when you was with the Indians?"

Esther winced at the reference. "Yes. Several hundred. Then, when I worked with Pastor Waite in the mission in New York, I delivered several hundred more. And I used the same herbs I'll be giving Abigail. Needless pain will only sap her strength."

Veraleen continued to regard Esther with suspicion. "Well, I say it's natural to hurt when a woman has a baby. Woman's burden is pain, and if the Good Lord had not a wanted it to hurt, He would not a made it hurt. He said to Eve right in the Good Book that we was to bring forth young'uns in sorrow. And the way I see it, it ain't proper to tamper with the Lord's way."

It amused Esther that Veraleen resented the idea of Abigail not having to suffer, and she suppressed a smile. "Veraleen, God made people with legs and feet for walking, but we ride in wagons or on horses every chance we get," Esther said easily. "It saves our energy for more important things."

Granny Cranney laughed boisterously, slapping her thighs with delight. "She's got you there, Vera!" she cackled. "She's sure got you there!"

The others smiled and chuckled, and Veraleen's thin pale features contracted into a dark frown and flushed an angry brick color. She turned and looked out the entrance, pretending to study something outside, then she closed the flap, shutting out any cool air.

Esther made a mental note that the drawn look of Veraleen's face and the way she sat with her shoulders hunched indicated a chronic stomach complaint. In fact, no doubt the older woman's gut was probably burning right now, like she had swallowed a hot coal.

"Your stomach bothers you a lot, doesn't it?" Esther said, feeling a boldness she had not experienced in the nine years since her rescue.

At the mention, a spasm hit, and Veraleen's hand knotted into a fist and ground at the spot just below her ribs. A glaze of sweat stood out on her upper lip, and her already sallow complexion turned dough-colored.

"You can really do somethin' to help this?" she asked in a pain-weakened voice.

Esther nodded. "After Abigail and her baby are comfortable, I'll stir up some herb tea for you."

Startled, the women exchanged glances. Granny peered into Esther's face. "How'd you know 'bout that? Vera do not complain none. We know 'cause we're family. But you, you ain't said more'n two words to any of us since you and your good Pastor joined the wagon train in Independence."

Esther restrained the temptation to remind them that it was they who had avoided her, and said instead, "I'm a healer, trained in the ways of herbs and massage. I can tell when people are in pain by the way they sit or walk or stand."

Veraleen stared at Esther, weighing her words, then with a tight smile, she said, "Then I'd be much obliged for somethin' to stop the burnin.' Been naggin' me a bit more lately than I'm used to," she confessed.

Esther gave a brief nod, then turned her full attention to Abigail. The skepticism with which the women regarded Esther slowly vanished and, silently, they looked from one to the other as though asking permission to speak. Finally, Delia said, "My youngest has a diaper rash that's turned to sores and blisters. Could you take a look at him?"

Esther raised her head and a shadow of a smile lifted her lips. "I'd be glad to. Show you how to wash your diapers to keep the rash away, too."

Ruth, a sister to Veraleen and married to a Cranney brother, moved self-consciously and cleared her throat. "My girl suffers terrible with her woman's time. Cramps and gets so weak and sick she cain't keep up on the trail and has to ride."

"I have just the thing for her. Make her forget her time's even here."

Granny cast a hesitant glance at Esther. "My good Mister's got such a crick in his back some days he can hardly hobble along, and he do not sleep much nights. Real wearin' on him, and I'm right worried he won't be strong enough to make it to Oregon." She dropped her eyes and smoothed at her stained apron. "My back hurts a mite, too, now and then."

"I imagine it hurts more than a mite," Esther said. "From the way you hitch along, I'd say it hurt a lot most days. I have something that will ease the pain. Won't cure your problem, but it will give relief."

Squinting her eyes and sizing up Esther carefully, she asked, "And what do you charge for all this kindness, Missy?"

Esther chuckled deep in her throat. "The charge is what you can afford. Supper and thanks have been my pay more often than not."

Granny smiled, showing wide gaps between her remaining teeth. "If you can deliver all the relief you say you can, I'll gladly give you supper and thanks here on the trail. But when we get to Oregon, I'll do better'n that!"

Veraleen grunted and heaved herself to her feet. "There ought to be some coffee left if the men ain't drunk it all. I'll go see if I can't scrape together a cup fer you and Jasmine. It's gonna be a long night from the way that girl's restin' between cramps."

While she was gone, the contractions picked up, each one harder than the last. It was time to gentle Abigail's pain.

Esther poured a dark liquid into a cup. "This tea will help," she promised. "I want you to unclench your teeth now so you can drink."

"Yes, Abigail, do as Esther says," Sister Waite spoke up, helping the laboring girl to a half-sitting position. "She's a healer, and we all believe in what she's doing." Her eyes narrowed dangerously as she turned to demand support from the women looking on with rapt attention.

Esther nearly fainted from the shock. Has God wrought a miracle after all these years?

While Abigail slowly sipped the bitter brew, the women relaxed and talked quietly among themselves. Then, after carefully returning the cup to the herb chest, Esther placed her hand on Abigail's thigh, feeling the tension drain away.

With Abigail relaxed for the moment, Esther leaned back in a more comfortable position and smothered a yawn, then blinked her eyes to resist the sleep threatening to close them.

Soon, another contraction began, and Esther sat forward. The pain built in intensity, and Esther rose to her knees and again rested her hand on Abigail's stomach to feel the rhythm of the spasms. Bending down close and speaking in a hushed voice, she instructed her when to breathe and when to push. When the contraction passed, Abigail collapsed like a rag doll.

"How long is this going to take?" she asked, gasping for breath, then letting out a healthy yell with the next contraction.

"You're coming nicely, Abigail," Esther reassured her. "You're doing just fine."

Just then, the tent entrance flapped open and Veraleen stepped through, carefully balancing two cups of steaming coffee. She handed one to Esther and the other to Sister

Waite. "Sounded like a right good one that time."

Grateful, Esther accepted the cup. "Yes, it won't be long now." Taking a sip of the fragrant brew, her head jerked up in surprise. "This is freshly made."

Veraleen blushed slightly and squirmed in embarrassment. "Tried to pour that stuff the men was drinkin'." She held her stomach and grunted as she lowered herself back onto the rock. "So strong it kinda oozed outta the pot like molasses. Were too thin to eat and warn't fit to drink."

Esther laughed and took another sip. "Sister Waite and I are much obliged to you for the trouble."

"Afraid it's us that's obliged to you. I do not know how little Abigail woulda done, this bein' her first young'un, if you had not a been willin' to help out."

Taking another sip of the scalding coffee, Esther smiled her gratitude.

Silence again settled over the tent, but it was not a restful silence. Esther sensed an agitation beneath it. Except for Granny who dozed with her chin resting on her chest and her lower lip drooping, the women were all alert.

Finally, Veraleen gave the little grunt that prefaced her every act and said, "We was uncommon rude to you, Esther, and we need to apologize."

"That's not necessary," Esther murmured.

"Oh, yes it is," Ruth and Delia chorused.

Their sincerity touched Esther deeply, and she fought to hold back the tears. These were the first white women in the years since her rescue who had reached out to her, had accepted her as anything but a healer to be called in time of need. "Thank you," she said in a trembling whisper, not trusting herself to say more.

Veraleen glared at Sister Waite and worked the muscles of

her jaw. Finally, she could contain her resentment no longer. "And while I'm about it, Sister Waite, I'd like to know how you'd get along with the Indians, was you to be took sudden into their midst?"

Sister Waite sat back on her heels and scowled. "I can assure you, I would not permit one of those filthy heathens to touch me." She paused in her tirade and glared sharply at Esther. "And as for a savage making me his wife, I would kill him or myself to prevent such a thing."

"But, Jasmine, dear, it's against the laws of God to take your own life or the life of another," Ruth reminded her gently.

Delia's young eyes grew wide. "I just can't think what I'd do if some Indian carried me off and threatened to—" She shuddered at the unspoken horror.

Granny, apparently feeling enough had been said on the subject, turned to Esther, and asked, "Tell us, child, 'bout your capture."

Since the women seemed genuinely interested in hearing about her ordeal and since she knew it would help pass the time for all of them, Esther told them much the same story she had shared with Savage earlier in the day. When she finished, she sat quietly observing Abigail.

"Ya got real sad eyes," Veraleen commented. "Ya sorry ya got rescued?"

Esther pursed her lips in thought before she replied. "It's painful to be considered an untouchable. People even refused to sit near me in church, so I often sat in a corner by myself. The only ones who did not mind conversing with me were those who did not know about my background and the women of the street where I worked with Pastor Waite. But when they learned I had been brought up by savages—" She paused, thinking of her new friend—the gentle man who bore that name— "then even the poorest souls in New York held themselves aloof from me as though I had committed sins that might rub off and poison them."

"Well, have ya?" Veraleen asked bluntly.

Esther could not hide her smile. "As an apprentice medicine woman, I was kept far too busy to get into trouble. I can lay claim to no more than the usual sins everyone is guilty of."

Sister Waite looked up, startled by Esther's story. "You never told us any of this."

"You never asked," Esther said softly and watched an ugly red stain creep up Jasmine's neck.

Handing the empty coffee cup to Delia and sitting forward again, Esther watched as Abigail tensed with the onset of another contraction. Every muscle in her body became rigid with the effort and a shrill, piercing scream filled the tent once more.

"Glory be!" Veraleen exclaimed, her eyes wide with delight. "That screech were pure beautiful."

"It hurts so," Abigail panted. "Is everything all right?"

"Abigail, you're going to deliver a healthy baby very soon," Esther said with a reassuring smile. "Be strong."

Two more contractions, a quick, competent move by Esther, and Ruth held up the lantern so all the women gathered round could see the newest little soul.

"Oh, Abigail, you've got the purtiest baby boy I ever seen!" Veraleen babbled.

Abigail gave a tired smile. "A boy," she sighed and relaxed.

The small face twisted, the mouth opened wide, and tiny arms flailed the air. He drew in his first breath, a deep gasp to

expand the lungs, and expelled the air in a loud wail. He drew
in another breath and wailed even louder, a lusty bellow that
filled the tent and spilled out into the night, and his firm little
body flushed pink with life and health.

A cheer went up outside as the men and children recognized the sound, and a deep voice bawled against the wall of
the tent. "What we got in there?"

Veraleen stuck her head through the tent flap. "We got us
the finest boy I ever seen, that's what we got. Joe, ya got
yerself a son!"

five

Glad to be useful at last, the Cranney women washed and dressed Abigail in her fresh shift and moved her to a clean pallet, while Esther gathered her things and left.

Seeking a quiet moment alone, she walked out into the cool evening air. The stars hung bright along the horizon, but in much of the sky, they were washed to nothingness by the brilliance of the Comanche moon. Esther did not recall ever being quite so aware of a full moon. It was bright enough to see the tiny feeding night creatures. Bone weary, she gave a prayer of thanks for the safe delivery of another baby, then slowly walked back to the camp.

Sinking into her bed underneath Pastor Waite's second wagon, Esther tried to sleep. In spite of her numbing weariness, all she managed to do, however, was to think of other bright moonlit nights and to grow homesick for her Indian family. When she had been in unfamiliar territory in New York City, the strangeness had kept such thoughts at bay. Here on the prairie, she found herself drawn more and more to thoughts of her early life with the Delaware.

Giving up on sleep, she took her mat and, seeking the peaceful serenity of the woods, carried it into the tangle of trees near the camp. Finding a level place under some berry bushes, she stretched out the pallet. This time before she lay down, she knelt in prayer. A deep sense of gratitude stirred in her at the latest miracle of childbirth, and she gave thanks, too, for the change in attitude among the women of the Cranney family. They would spread the word, and perhaps

Esther would be accepted by the rest of the women in the train. Wearily she curled onto the pallet as sleep swept her away on gentle arms.

Hidden by the thicket of berry bushes at the foot of pecan and walnut trees blooming their promise of a bounteous fall harvest, Esther awoke, taking a moment to remember where she was and why. In these few minutes of respite before she rose to see how Abigail and the baby had fared during the remainder of the night, Esther savored the fragrance of the blooms mingled with the new grass. Solitude was frowned upon when there was work to be done, and there was always work when the wagon train halted.

Enoch had said that if they went the night without being attacked, they would stop here to allow Abigail time to recover a bit and wait for Savage to return with the army. Because there was wood and water, they could wash their clothes and themselves, and repair the wagons and harnesses in readiness for the hard trail ahead.

Esther closed her eyes and let the fragrant breeze blow over her, felt the tender shoots of grass caress her cheeks, allowed her tired body to sink into the bed of last fall's leaves, growing pungent with the warming of the early May morning. Her thoughts drifted off on the shredded clouds, floating in tattered wisps across the azure sky. Times like now when she gave her mind free rein, her memory stirred with visions of those warm, carefree times with Walking Bear and her Indian family, when she had felt completely loved and fully accepted.

Hearing something, Esther stiffened. The sound was not like anything she normally heard. This sound traveled from a great distance and vibrated against her ear next to the ground, like a great drum beating inside the earth. All her senses came alive, and she pressed her head more tightly on the hard-packed dirt. The sound thrummed with pulsing regularity, growing closer and louder as she listened. What could it mean?

In this strange new land where tall grass rolled on forever, pushed into waves dappled with primroses by the eternal wind, Esther had come to expect anything. But this throbbing earth was different, frightening. Should she sound an alarm? And if so, what would she say? The ground beats beneath my ear? Pastor Waite would laugh and make fun of her for a week over such nonsense. No, she would not risk such ridicule. Better to wait until she had something visible to report.

With body taut and every nerve tingling, Esther listened as the drumming sound rolled deeper and louder in the direction of the circled wagons. Now the ground under her began vibrating ever so slightly with the rhythm, making cold chills prick along her arms.

Suspended in a web of growing fear, time held little meaning, and Esther had no idea how long she remained motionless until the sound waves began traveling through the air, also. At first it imitated distant thunder, but as the rumble drew closer and louder, the vibrations took on an increased intensity and a chant of voices rose above the thunder.

"Indians!" a woman's terrified scream richocheted through the camp.

Suddenly everything came together in a crescendo of noise and light. Galloping hard over the low hills behind the copse of trees and into Esther's view was a band of Indians on horseback.

Quickly, she raised herself to a sitting position, ready to run. Then she shrank back down. Too late! For fear of ridicule, she had waited too long. Bedlam broke loose in the camp as mothers screamed for their children still playing down by the river, and men raced for their guns.

Without any visible signal to the animal, the chief stopped his raven-black pony and turned so that Esther, still hidden in the bushes, could see his face slashed with bright yellow paint extending down onto his breast. Circles of black around his eyes, accented with smaller smears of red, made his face terrible to behold.

The Indian sat atop his quivering black stallion with a relaxed grace acquired from years of riding, his long lean legs encased in soft, tan leggings decorated with deep fringe and tinkling brass bells. Except for the quiver of arrows strapped across the smooth thick muscles, his upper body was bare. A wine-colored breechclout fluttered behind him in the hot wind like a bloodied flag.

Tall and lordly on his sleek horse, the war chief rode up to the first wagon where Enoch stood, looking no less frightened than the greenest of his charges. Dangling from the chief's left hand was a soiled white scrap of fabric, nearly dragging the ground and rippling weakly in the slight breeze. At least, Esther thought, this symbol meant they came in peace.

Scores of painted Comanche warriors on winded ponies joined their leader and milled behind him, churning the prairie to dust. Sullen and suspicious, their heads constantly swept from side to side, their sharp slitted eyes missing nothing.

As the band of marauders fixed the group with their venomous looks, all activity and sound ceased. People froze in place—a large hammy hand reaching for the gun leaning against a wagon wheel remained poised in mid-air; a mother attempting to hide her small child under her skirts paused with the skirt raised nearly to her knees, the little boy crouched at her feet, unmoving.

Esther, well hidden in her woodsy retreat and unseen by the invaders, remained fixed, looking to the tent where Abigail lay helpless. The leader raised his left hand and opened his fingers. Esther's eyes fastened on the white flag as it fluttered slowly to the ground and disappeared into the dust under the prancing feet of the leader's nervous mount. They had not come in peace, after all. Her heart thundered with panic.

The warriors watched in silence as Enoch Fisher stepped forward toward the waiting war chief. Foreboding welled in Esther's chest, scarcely giving her heart room to beat. But beat it did, pounding in her ears, rocking her body with its force. While she was not satisfied with her life as a former Indian hostage, she did not relish the thought of being captured again. The first time she had been a child. Now, as a woman, her treatment would be quite different.

Inside the circle, Pastor Waite disengaged himself from the frightened flock clustered around him and walked slowly from between the wagons, joining Enoch. Together, they moved with slow deliberate steps toward the waiting Indians.

The heavy silence, broken only by the occasional stamp and whinny of an impatient pony, drew nerves taut. Suddenly, the tent flap swished open and Jasmine, who had been left to tend Abigail and her baby, stormed outside. "Where's that bucket of wat . . ." she began and swallowed her words. Her face paled until, under the blazing sun, she appeared to have no features at all except for her great wide eyes. She froze in midstep, staring in terrified silence at the hideously painted and fully armed Indians.

The ponies, having caught their breath, quieted. No one spoke and, with the passing moments, the silence grew thicker and thicker, like syrup boiling down.

The chief peered intently at each woman, apparently searching for someone or something. Esther shrank farther into the shelter of the shadowy bushes under which she had slept and prayed he would not see her there. *But Thy will is mine, O Lord.*

The breeze stirred, twirling the feathers on the Comanches' slender lances, raised in a nonthreatening position. A war pony whinnied and, from inside the wagon corral, Pastor Waite's sorrel answered. The Indian pony danced at the response causing the small brass cones on his rider's leggings to jingle merrily.

A movement inside the wagon circle caught Esther's eye. She clenched her hands into fists, pressing them against her lips to keep back the scream threatening to erupt as she recognized Joseph Cranney easing along the circle. He carried his new breechloader, a wonderful new weapon he could load over three times in one minute. Ever since leaving Independence, Joseph had practiced continually for just such a moment as this.

A hundred Indians, and he could kill three a minute! With the ludicrous thought, the urge to scream died and Esther fought against hysterical laughter bubbling inside.

At last, Pastor Waite stepped forward, and he and the Comanche war chief, still sitting in regal disdain atop his horse, began talking. When neither could understand the other, Enoch stepped up to intercede. Using the sign language of all the Plains Indians, he explained who the people in the train were and what they were doing here so far off the usual wagon routes.

The chief considered Enoch's information, then turned and spoke to his men in short clipped words. They seemed to be pondering their course of action.

At last, the leader signed to Enoch to gather all his people before the Comanches. Enoch knew all about these wildly painted warriors and their warring raids on the Texas settlements, and he hesitated. The lances dropped with swift precision to striking position.

Give them what they want, Esther pleaded silently. If you do not give them what they desire, they will surely take it and give no thought to the cost.

Pastor Waite gave the signal and, slowly, people came from all directions. The older children grouped together into a frightened huddle near the wagon. The men filed in from various places about the encampment to stand in back of Enoch and Pastor Waite. The women, clucking at the little ones to hurry along, formed a ragged line behind their men.

"Is this all?" the war chief signed.

Pastor Waite turned and looked over the assemblage. "Joseph!" he called. "Esther! These good men mean us no harm. Hurry along, now."

Reluctantly, Joseph slid through a break in the circle between the two front wagons, the unplaned wood of the wagon boxes plucking at his thick cotton shirt. Then he stopped, glaring his hatred of the large band assembled before him and fingering the blue-black trigger of his weapon.

"Joseph, come here at once," Enoch insisted, ignoring the young man's hesitation.

Obediently, Esther rose from her spot in the island of trees and gathered up her pallet. No one took notice of her, camouflaged as she was by dappled sunlight and swaying shadows. All eyes were fixed on Joseph's gun.

The war chief reached out a hand, gesturing that he wanted the rifle. But Joseph pulled the weapon tightly against his chest. A dangerous twist curled the chief's lips and his eyes took on a deadly glitter.

Seeing the chief's ominous expression, Enoch stepped toward the towering young farmer. "Joseph, give the man your gun," he ordered as if speaking to a wayward child.

Still Joseph clutched the weapon to him, giving no indication that he had any intention of parting with his most precious possession. The war chief remained motionless, hand extended.

To the chief's left, a tall man with a jagged scar carved across his face glanced first at his leader, then at Joseph. When Joseph showed no signs of relinquishing his rifle, the warrior pulled back his lance. In the brilliant sunlight, the taut muscles bulged and flexed as he shifted his fingers along the long thin shaft to locate the perfect balance. Joseph, unmoving in his terror, stared transfixed at the tip of the delicate weapon aimed at him.

Reaching out, Enoch jerked the gun from Joseph's grip and handed it up to the war chief. Looking it over carefully, the chief signed for instructions on how to use the weapon and, reluctantly, Enoch took back the rifle and demonstrated. Joseph looked on helplessly, fury twisting his face as the war chief slipped the strap over his shoulder and gave the gun an affectionate pat.

Driven to desperation, Joseph leaped toward the Indian. But at that moment, Enoch Fisher's hand shot out and caught the younger man across the chest, sending him spinning to the ground. Then, to make sure he stayed there, Enoch placed a foot in his midsection, pinning him down. Thoroughly humbled by his spread-eagle position, Joseph lay still, but his eyes flashed pure hatred.

"Esther!" Pastor Waite called again.

She stepped from the sheltering copse and all heads turned to watch her slow progression across the prairie, her tall, lithe body flowing with an untaught grace. The Comanche leader's eyes narrowed to slits as she walked, head erect and shoulders squared, moving in long easy strides toward him.

Having just awakened, Esther had not had time to braid her hair and anchor it to her head. Flaxen strands of silk cascaded over her shoulders and down her back, rippling in the morning breeze.

Head still high, she came to a halt beside Enoch and a discreet distance from the powerful black horse. Her eyes never wavered from the chief's face as she stood, mute, before him. Though she was quaking with fright on the inside, Esther had learned in her fifteen years with the Indians that showing any fear often provoked the creation of ingenious tortures. So her own expression remained mask-like.

The war chief handed his lance to one of his men, swung his leg over the horse's neck, and slid easily to the ground, flexing gracefully up on his toes. Then he sauntered casually up to Esther, his hooded black eyes piercing in their intensity. Everyone, white and Indian alike, seemed to hold their breath as they watched the meeting between the two. Presently the chief signed something.

"Says his name is Running Elk," Esther translated, paling noticeably.

"That means something to you, doesn't it?" she asked, keeping her voice low.

Enoch wiped a trembling hand over his mouth. "Means he's the most powerful of the Comanche war chiefs."

"How fortunate," Esther said, attempting a smile. "At least we do not attract the socially undesirable."

Despite the situation, Enoch gave a weak chuckle. "You got guts, girl. I'll hand ya that."

"You forget that I've been captured before, if that's what they're planning."

Her reminder had an instant sobering effect on Enoch. "I'm plumb sorry, Miss Esther. Did not mean to make light."

"I did. When you're scared to death and hope seems remote, laughter sometimes drives out the fear."

All the while she and Enoch bantered, Running Elk was appraising Esther, omitting no part of her person from his intense scrutiny. Then he stepped next to her and ran strong fingers through the soft strands of her hair. She froze. Did he mean to scalp her? Without warning, he gave a tug.

Esther's eyes flashed. She grabbed his hand and flung it away from her. "What do you think you're doing?" she demanded with far more bravado than she felt. She would let Enoch sign her words.

At her rash action, a gasp went up from the crowd.

A slow grin, parting strong white teeth, altered the chief's countenance. He signed.

"Just wanted to see if it was attached to her head," Enoch explained to the stricken group. "He did not mean to cause her no pain."

Esther let her eyes stray to the fresh scalps twisting from the lance poles. "Do you have a painless plan for scalping me?" she asked, making her voice calm and cold.

The smile faded from Running Elk's face, and he demanded of Enoch to know what she had said. When Enoch told him, Running Elk let loose a roar of laughter.

He signed, "I have no wish to have your hair any place but where it is. It floats about you like moonlight. I only tested to assure myself it was real."

Intently, he watched for her reaction to his words, and it gradually occurred to Esther that the man had shown no interest in anyone but her. In some way she was responsible for this raid, and suddenly she knew that she held the key to the safety of everyone in the entire wagon train. Her insides knotted with the dread realization that she was to become an Indian hostage once again.

The rest of the Comanche raiding party sat silently on round-bellied ponies, stomping their restlessness into the dirt. The wind ruffled the brightly colored feathers and pieces of cloth attached to the warriors' shields and lances, lending a strangely festive air to the deadly moments. Esther lost track of time as Running Elk, without speaking further, gently fingered her hair and let his eyes roam her face and form.

When it appeared that they were going to stand thus through the day, one of the Comanches spoke briefly in the hard chunking syllables of their language.

Acknowledging his warrior, Running Elk nodded and motioned Esther toward his horse, in much the same manner a gentleman would indicate the carriage was waiting. Esther, not quite resigned to her fate, stumbled in her first step, and he reached out a hand to steady her as she walked with slow measured tread into an unknown future.

Lifting Esther onto the horse with no more effort than if she had been a child, Running Elk sprang up behind her and wrapped a possessive arm around her waist, pulling her tightly against his chest. "You stay quiet and not move," he said firmly to her in Comanche.

Though she did not understand all the words, his meaning was clear. She nodded and sat stiff as a pole in the saddle.

Satisfied that Esther understood what he expected of her, Running Elk signed to the group.

"What did he say?" Pastor Waite asked when the message was finished.

Enoch turned so all the company could hear. "Running Elk says all he wants is the golden-haired one. They've raided enough and are itchin' to get back to their warm lodges in the north. If we won't make no foolish moves, they'll leave peacefullike." He turned anguished eyes on Esther, and his shoulders drooped with the helplessness he felt. "I'm plumb sorry, Miss Esther."

Though inside she felt a chill, Esther kept any emotion from her face as Running Elk slid off the pony and tied her ankles with a rope passed under the horse's belly. "If my capture will spare the lives of but one of you, I go willingly," she said. "I do have one request, though.

Enoch, go get my Bible and my herb case, please."

His anxious eyes on Running Elk, Enoch signed her request. Running Elk nodded and said something to the tall scar-faced warrior next to him. The man leaped from his pony and strode up to Enoch. More signing.

"Where do you keep them, daughter?" Pastor Waite asked, keeping a wary eye on the Indians.

"In my trunk in the second wagon."

Before anyone else could move, there was a blur of calico, and Esther watched Jasmine dash toward the wagon. The Comanche warrior sprinted after her, snaked out an arm, and hauled her up short. Jasmine landed a solid kick on his shin. He let out a roar of pain and threw her to the ground. Frantically, Enoch signed that Jasmine was only going after the things Esther had asked for. Though Running Elk nodded in understanding, he growled his displeasure of Jasmine's treatment of the Indian, now limping about on his injured leg.

With further ado, Jasmine clambered over the tailgate and into the wagon. A few seconds of rustling and she reappeared, holding the small trunk out for the Indian to take. Grudgingly he reached up and grabbed it, then waited for Jasmine to climb down. They stood eyeing one another, but Jasmine did not drop her gaze.

Good for you, Esther applauded silently, recognizing a side of the red-haired woman that neither she nor anyone else had ever seen. Their amazement registered even over the fear on their faces.

Clipped words from the warrior, and Running Elk nodded again.

Carrying Esther's trunk, the warrior handed it to one of the other men. "Please be careful," she signed. "There is much magic in that case."

A flicker of alarm altered the expressions of the Indians, and the unfortunate brave who was holding the case at the moment started as if he held fire in the palm of his hand.

"No, no," Esther signed quickly. "It is good magic. Magic to take away sickness and pain."

The raiding party relaxed visibly, and cheered by Esther's smile, the brave sat tall, pleased with the honor of guarding the precious container.

A shrill scream split the silence, and Esther whirled to see the Indian who had followed Jasmine, packing her like a sack of flour toward his horse.

Pastor Waite blanched and thundered, "Unhand her, you heathen savage!"

"What do you think you are doing?" Esther flared at Running Elk, signing her words. "It is one thing to take me. It is quite another to take Jasmine hostage."

He laughed and signed, "Tall Lance is as attracted to Jasmine as I am to you. Keep out of this matter. It is not your concern."

Tall Lance dumped Jasmine on his horse, where she immediately fought to get down. Seeing her struggle, several warriors dismounted and helped Tall Lance lash Jasmine's ankles together with ropes passed under the horse's belly in the same manner Esther was tied to Running Elk's horse. All the time they worked, she flailed at them with her fists and screamed at the top of her lungs.

Her feet secured, Tall Lance produced a leather thong, bound her wrists together, and fastened that to the saddle. Jasmine continued screaming and hollering dire threats while he worked. In her exertion, her hair worked loose and now fell over her shoulders and down her back in a flaming fall of satin.

Tall Lance stood with his hands on his hips, staring at her. Then, he looked at Running Elk, smiled, and made a guttural comment.

Running Elk laughed, then sobered immediately. He began signing, this time with an emotion Esther understood well.

"The Comanche have what they come for and are leavin' now," Enoch translated. "There won't be no trouble 'less we make it. Still if any of ye want war, I expect they'd be glad to oblige." He stopped and fixed the company with a glacial stare. "I say that if any one of ye plans on bein' a hero, ye'd best be prepared to sentence the whole shebang to a grisly death. If these fellers look calm, it's only because they've gotten their fill of blood . . . for now. But that do not mean they could not turn cruel without warnin'. They're also tellin' us to break camp and move on. At nightfall, Runnin' Elk will send back a scout. If he finds us, they'll attack."

Wordlessly, fear-glazed faces nodded their agreement to the terms, and Enoch turned and signed their intent to let the Comanches ride peacefully away.

Esther settled in front of her captor on the horse and smelled the familiar combination of smoke and tallow and leather emanating from him. A flood of memories swept over her, memories she had buried deep as she tried to forget her other life.

Making her backbone ramrod stiff, she held herself away from him. But when he quirted his horse, she lurched. Once more he wrapped a sinewy arm around her waist and pulled her tightly against his chest.

Not trusting the white men, the warriors regrouped around Running Elk and Tall Lance. Then, bending low over their mounts, they galloped through hock-high grass and flowers to the northeast, up to the crest of a hill. There, Running Elk paused for one brief moment against the skyline.

Esther looked back at the big circle of white tops. From this distance, the people resembled ants as they scurried to break camp.

Dear Lord, she prayed. *Please go with Jasmine and me, and be with Savage as he comes for us.* Without question, she knew neither of them would disappoint her.

A quiet stole into her heart, leaving Esther free to concentrate on sitting with rigid spine, as far away from any contact with her abductor as she could manage.

Sensing her distaste, Running Elk pulled her hard against him, nearly squeezing the breath from her. Then, the great Comanche war chief sent his steed plunging over the hill and, for the second time in her life, Esther disappeared into the world of the People.

six

Fort Leavenworth, standing alone on the west bank of the Missouri River near the mouth of the Little Platte, broke the monotony of the rolling prairie, drawing the eye of the traveler and holding it like a rare coin in the palm of a hand. But today the sprawling encampment more nearly resembled a mirage, shimmering in the unseasonable heat of the May afternoon. Though the mountains, too far west to be visible, cooled the breeze sweeping across the plain, the sunbaked ground warmed it again before it had traveled any distance.

Lulled into lethargy by the mounting temperature, the guards on duty inside the gate lounged against the rock wall enclosing and securing the fort until the drumming of hooves in the distance brought them to life. Racing to the gun slits facing the plains, two young recruits shoved their Henry rifles through the openings and pulled back the hammers. Shivering in spite of the heat, they waited in tense anticipation.

"Open the gates!" shouted the sentry in the watchtower.

Quickly the soldiers swung wide the gate to Fort Leavenworth and stepped aside as the lone rider streaked in a straight line for the opening.

"Trouble!" one said.

"How do you know?" asked the other, new to the frontier.

"Indian signal for sounding an alarm is a rider aiming straight for the village. If there's no problem, he'll zigzag his way in. Savage always uses it."

"Could not ride any straighter than he is today. Wonder what's up?"

"We'll ask him when he dismounts."

But the Army scout, his buckskins covered with sweat, galloped past the guards in a cloud of dust and up to the hitching rack in front of the headquarters building. He jumped off his still-moving horse and raced up the stairs, forcing his way past Sergeant Major Archibald Haskell's desk in the outer room.

With a loud protest, Sergeant Haskell leaped to his feet and followed hard on Savage's heels. Ignoring the irate sergeant, Savage continued across the room with long quick steps, threw open the door, and marched unannounced into Colonel Mallory's office.

The tall slightly round-shouldered colonel looked up over a sheaf of papers, an angry red flushing his pale cheeks. "What is the meaning of this intrusion, Sergeant?" Colonel Mallory asked sharply, ignoring Savage. "I gave specific orders not to be disturbed until I complete this field report for Washington."

"Yes, sir. I know, sir," Sergeant Haskell hastily agreed. "But Savage took me by surprise, sir. Do you want me to show him out?" The sergeant glared his annoyance with the interruption. "I can boot him into the parade ground for you, sir."

The sudden unexpected sound of chuckling drew their attention to the dust-covered, foam-flecked scout leaning against the wall, his arms folded across his massive chest.

"When you two get through deciding if you'll hear my story, let me know." Savage shoved off from the white-washed wall with calculated deliberation, leaving a stain where his shoulder had rested. Then, as he sauntered to the center of the room, he brushed against the fastidious sergeant, marking his dark blue jacket with a smudge of dust.

Sergeant Haskell, a large burly army regular in the last years of his service, bristled and flicked the dust away in Savage's direction.

The colonel drew himself inside his own meticulous dress uniform, narrowed his eyes, and squinted his displeasure at Savage. *The man defied all sense of order and decency,* he thought. Why, in those dusty buckskins, he looked more Indian than military. He spoke his mind without deference to rank, took exception to his superior's orders any time it suited his fancy, and probably even indulged in all manner of sinful practices in his off-duty hours as well. Brook Savage was utterly contemptible!

Clasping his saber meaningfully, Colonel Mallory spoke from between clenched teeth. "You know, Mr. Savage, the only thing that makes your insolence the remotest bit tolerable is the fact that you are the best scout west of the Mississippi. If it were not for that, I would find countless reasons to have you court-martialed."

Savage broke into a rich full laugh. "I'd have to be a member of the Army for you to do that," he taunted. "So you'd better prepare to wait 'til Judgment Day!"

The colonel glared at Savage, swallowed over a fierce frown, and opened his mouth to speak again. But, when he caught sight of the mocking gray eyes, he apparently thought better of it, for his jaws snapped shut. Although the colonel was not a man ruled by his emotions, he came as close today as he ever had to hating Brook Savage.

He drew a deep breath, compressed his lips into a tight line, and continued to glower. "There is no excuse for such unmilitary behavior, Savage," he said in a thinly controlled voice. "You *were* hired by the U. S. Army. That makes you an employee of the government, *my* employee."

Ignoring the colonel and the sergeant, Savage strolled the rest of the way across the room and pulled up a stiff-backed chair near Colonel Mallory's desk. Swinging his leg over the top, carelessly he dropped into it. He removed his tan plains hat and beat it on the leg of the chair, then replaced it at an angle down over his eyes. Dust flew in clouds, settling in a gritty film on the writing paper strewn over the desk.

Seeing his precious report sullied, the colonel stopped pacing and dashed to rescue the once-white sheets, shoving them for safekeeping into a drawer. Then, shutting the drawer with some force, he sputtered, "Well, what did you want to tell me that was so important you could not wait to be announced?"

When Savage did not respond, Colonel Mallory gave the desk a sharp rap. Savage opened one eye and peered out from under his hat as the colonel sat in the chair behind the desk, winced, and with long graceful fingers, pressed his temples.

Poor dumb biscuit, Savage thought in a rare moment of compassion. *He makes life unnecessarily tough on himself, and then when he can't handle the mess he makes, he gets a sick headache so he can escape to the safe world inside his darkened bedroom.*

"Mr. Savage, are you, or are you not, going to tell me what message you bring?" The colonel drummed his fingers on the polished mahogany of the desktop.

Savage tipped his hat back and sat forward. He had had his fun, and there was not any more time to waste or it would be too late. In a voice raspy from dust and lack of sleep he said, far more calmly than he felt, "The young bucks on both sides are restless after the long winter. The Comanche and the

Cheyenne have cooked up some imagined insults and are planning to defend their honor in a couple of days."

Colonel Mallory slapped the desk with the palm of his hand and jumped to his feet. "Good heavens, man! You surely did not ride here in a frenzy to tell me that bit of news, if news it be. That's a normal day in the lives of those heathens."

His flash of charity gone, Savage ached to tell the colonel what he really thought of him, but now was not the proper time. If the pompous donkey would only listen, Savage might manage to hold his temper and chalk up another day without their coming to blows. "I agree there's nothing shocking about Indians warring among themselves, but I thought you might like to know that the wagon train I told you about earlier, possibly a hundred people strong, is camped smack in the middle of the proposed battleground. They're waiting on a birthing and, with water close by and the weather warm, they do not seem to be in much of a hurry to move on."

Colonel Mallory creased his untanned forehead into deep furrows and rubbed his temples again. "This news comes at a most inopportune time. As you know, most the men are on scouting missions, and we are severely understaffed."

Savage leaned forward. "If they're doing any scouting at all, they're going to see the gathering of the warriors and get back here on the double."

"I expect them before nightfall."

"Colonel, that could be too late. The moon will be full tonight, and you know what that means to the Comanche. Are you willing to gamble the lives of all those people?" Savage paused, feeling a twinge of pain. He cared about the others, but it was Esther he did not want to lose, not when he had just found her.

"Did you talk to the wagon master and tell him of the danger?"

The colonel's sarcastic question jerked Savage back to the present, and he ground his teeth to keep his temper in check. "I spoke to him," he managed to say in a quiet conversational tone, though the blood pounded in his temples from the desire to slam out of this stuffy little office and never come back. "Name's Enoch Fisher. But I did not know about the gathering of the tribes until I was on my way back here. If I had known, there still was not anything I could accomplish there alone. They need a troop escort."

Colonel Mallory picked up a book of Army regulations, leafed through a few pages, then flung it down. "It's no secret around here that I run this command post by the book. My first duty is to protect the fort . . . you know that, Savage. There *is* a purpose for rules and regulations."

"And some rules are made to be broken!" Savage snapped, tiring of their perpetual verbal swordplay. He felt sorry for the inept man, but he was not going to let the colonel "regulation" his way out of this one. "If any harm befalls those people in that wagon train, Colonel," he continued in a menacing tone, "I guarantee that you will be held personally accountable. Would not look good on your record when you come up for promotion, now would it? Would not look good at all." He waited, allowing the significance of his implication to sink home. "I really think you ought to send some troops out as soon as possible."

The colonel's face turned an unhealthy purple, and his eyes bugged dangerously. Dropping into his high-backed wooden chair, he sat stiffly on the edge of the seat. "Mr. Savage," he began icily, his Adam's apple bobbing with agitation, "*I* am in charge here. The men will leave when and *if* I say so and not one second before. I repeat, my first duty is the safety of this fort. If the Indians are going to war, I will not risk leaving the fort unprotected. We will wait until all the men have returned."

"That your final word?" Savage asked quietly, though he knew it was.

"Good day, Mr. Savage," Colonel Mallory said firmly, and retrieved his report from the desk drawer, thus dismissing both Savage and Sergeant Haskell.

It was late afternoon by the time Sergeant Haskell could talk the colonel into releasing the troops. At dusk the cavalry set out with Savage in the lead. He turned and looked over the sullen soldiers trailing out behind him. They had ridden most of the day, seen nothing, and come back to the fort anticipating a hot supper and some shut-eye. At Savage's insistence, they had been forced into this night ride. He would be lucky one of them did not shoot him in the back before it was over.

Savage squinted into the last rays of the dying sun, took a deep breath of the dry air, and choked. His throat felt tight, constricted. In another man, such symptoms might signal the onset of a cold. To Savage, who had never had a cold in his life, it meant death stalked his heels. He knew that what he felt, sensed, tasted was raw instinct, something most white men knew nothing about.

It was thanks to the Sioux and Cheyenne that Savage understood how necessary instinct was for survival. Years ago he had learned to listen to his instincts. They were given by God to protect His children, and though Savage was not big on praying, he did give daily thanks for the preservation of that gift.

His eyes began to burn, and he rubbed them with sweaty palms. He cleared his throat and took a swig of cool water from the canteen tied to the side of his saddle. Nothing eased the burning. He tried clearing his throat again and told himself how stupid Colonel Mallory was. The man was a coward and a donkey. He would let a wagon train be needlessly massacred and stay in his office making a report about it rather than face up to his responsibilities.

On they rode. Savage sighed, and wiped beads of perspiration from his forehead with the sleeve of the cotton shirt he had changed into out of deference to the heat.

Why did the Army always promote the most inept? he fumed inwardly. They came West, spewed out of the Academy, all alike from their starched uniforms and book-learned field tactics to the ambitious gleam in their eyes. With no exceptions, they were inexperienced, lacking understanding of the problems they faced, and with no desire to learn. All they cared about was upholding their precious traditions, following regulations to the letter. No deviations regardless of the circumstances.

And then they met Savage. He had to admit he enjoyed frustrating them. It was his way of getting even for their insensitive handling of delicate situations, their total ignorance of the problems to begin with. Savage had a much deeper reason for tormenting the officers, however. He was an individualist and restrictions infuriated him. The Army was no place for him. If he had not made a pledge to his dying adoptive Indian mother to help keep the peace, he would never again enter a fort.

Having been born in the West when few white men were even aware it existed, he felt uncomfortable even in the small settlements beginning to spring up along the eastern edge of the territory. Given his preference, he would never choose to leave the majestic snow-capped mountains where he had learned the frontier skills with his father, one of the most knowledgeable of mountain men. In the land of the Cheyenne and Sioux, the pine-scented air filled his lungs and blew cool against his beardless cheeks. By the time he was eight, he had even learned to speak reasonably well the language of the People and could sign with great skill.

Then, to the boundless joy of his New York-born mother, when he was ten, they had found a small white settlement and moved into their first permanent house. Savage rubbed the tips of his fingers lightly over the scars on his face, remembering the terrible sickness that had snatched her away forever and nearly killed him.

After he recovered, he and his father had traveled the high country together until the fall of his eleventh year, when his father had been shot by the Sioux during a war between the tribes, such as was now brewing. Savage was captured.

He learned a great deal about the wilderness from the Sioux, and the Cheyenne taught him the rest—at this point, his memories grew more obscure, more resistant to being called forth from the recesses of his mind. Even after all these years, he could not think of Smiles Alot without grieving for his Indian wife, his two beautiful children—nor had he considered taking another wife . . . until he looked into the eyes of Esther Wheeler this morning.

With every thought, Savage ached with the loveliness of her, this princess of the prairie he had come upon so unexpectedly, all gold and ivory and azure blue. Those eyes—large and luminous and vividly blue—reminded him of a crisp, clear autumn sky, and they were as distant, as ancient, as inscrutable. He guessed that when she chose, those same eyes could turn to glittering ice or to blue fire . . . .

Sergeant Haskell uttered an oath, bringing Savage back from his musings with a jolt. It had grown dark hours ago, but the moon made tracking at night easy. They had just ridden over a hill Savage had described in considerable detail as a likely place to camp if Abigail decided to have her baby and the train was forced to stop for some time. But there was no wagon train to be seen.

Savage set spurs to his horse, and he and the sergeant raced to the site. Swinging out of the saddle, Savage knelt to survey the pulverized earth.

"Looks like they were here and pulled out in a hurry," Sergeant Haskell observed as he kicked at an abandoned crate of chickens clucking wildly.

A blind man could have arrived at that conclusion, Haskell, Savage thought sourly as he tossed a buffalo chip into the firepit and watched tiny red sparks spin off into the wind.

Using the firepit as the center, he began walking in ever-widening circles until he found what he was looking for. A large number of unshod horses had milled around this spot, but there had been no struggle. He removed his hat and scratched his head. The men in the train were armed, and they were not cowards, that much he knew. If they had been threatened, they would have put up a fight, yet there was no sign of a struggle.

Then, he saw it . . . a once-white piece of cloth trampled into the dirt by sharp hooves. He picked it up and shook out the shredded flag of truce. His shoulders sagged as he tried to piece together what had happened. Riding into a camp under the peace flag was an old trick, but then the Indians usually went wild. Obviously, this group had not done that.

Savage found the footprints where the children had clustered, the line of tracks made by the women and men. He even located two sets of prints at the front, set apart from the group. Most likely Enoch and that Pastor what's-his-name.

Nothing made sense. All the Indian pony tracks headed northeast, but the wagon train continued on northwest. The settlers had not been followed.

Then something hit Savage in the pit of his stomach. It drove through him, sending him into a frenzy, a feeling he could not ignore . . . not when he had ridden all day with the smell of death nearly choking him.

"All right, Sergeant, have the men mount up," Savage ordered. "Let's go find that wagon train . . . if there's anything left of it."

seven

Esther forced everything from her mind, refusing to think of the ride ahead, of the night at the end of the day, and of what was surely in store for her. She concentrated instead on mundane things like the sun beating hot on her unprotected head and the growing thirst that gradually was becoming a torment. She wondered how Running Elk stood it, for though he had an army canteen tied to his saddle and she could hear water sloshing inside, he never touched it. At least, as a captive of eastern Indians, there was always water, and one was allowed to drink if one gave no trouble. Here, it seemed, no one, not even the most powerful of the warriors, quenched their thirst.

Jasmine continued behaving badly. Her hands, bound to the rounded pommel of the saddle, chafed and bled in her attempts to free herself. She alternately screamed and cried until Tall Lance, his disfiguring scar growing white with anger, finally tied a noose around her neck to silence her. Choked by the thin leather line, Jasmine's face turned a frightening shade of purple as she gagged and gasped for air. Each time she seemed about to lose consciousness, Tall Lance would loosen the thong. But instead of being grateful, Jasmine railed at him until he was forced to cinch it tight again, leaving the noose so she could draw in only enough air to sustain life.

Esther could see the coarse horsehair lariat that bound Jasmine's feet and left harsh red circles around each ankle. Blood trickled over her bare, swollen feet. Esther was sure her own feet and ankles must look the same, but since they had long ago gone numb, there was no way to tell for sure.

They rode like this for hours, it seemed. Then, without warning, a shrill, gurgling scream pierced the stillness. It was Jasmine. Apparently the leather of the thong around her neck had become sweat-soaked and stretched, for suddenly she launched into another violent tirade.

"May I speak to her?" Esther signed to Running Elk.

Running Elk looked intently at Esther, then nodded. "Tall Lance!" he said, his voice issuing the name as a command.

His arm in midair ready to strike a blow, Tall Lance glanced over his shoulder, his puzzlement at the unexpected interruption showing in his twisting mouth and the questioning look sparking behind black eyes.

"The golden-haired one requests to speak with your woman. Perhaps she can make her behave."

Tall Lance took the measure of Esther, letting his eyes penetrate deep into hers. At last he nodded. "Let her know that I will put up with very little more, then I become angry," Tall Lance signed, his face flushed dark red under the pecan coloring.

Esther wondered what he would be like if he were not making some effort to control his temper. "Jasmine!" she shouted above the woman's screams. "Listen to me!" she ordered sharply.

Jasmine paid Esther no mind, but continued to wail in deafening volume.

"Jasmine, you are going to be killed if you do not hush this minute!"

Jasmine stopped and sucked in a deep breath that rattled over her swollen throat. "Let them kill me." She spat the words in a hoarse croak and glared at Tall Lance with eyes moss-green with hatred. "It will be preferable to what I am suffering," she ended in an ear-splitting wail.

Esther felt a great urge to shake her. "Jasmine, you do not begin to know what you are saying. You won't be killed with the neat stroke of a knife or arrow. Tall Lance will . . . well, you do not want to hear what *he* will do." Esther paused and saw the fury seething in Tall Lance's eyes, waiting for her words to sink into Jasmine's head.

Apparently Jasmine heard and believed, for she stopped screaming, and the very air seemed to sigh with relief. Then, unexpectedly, she let out such a shriek that Esther felt Running Elk tense. The unearthly noise startled the horses, and they pranced nervously, their heads rearing. It took a minute to quiet them before Jasmine croaked in angry ragged sounds, "They would not dare! I'll bite and kick and scratch—"

Esther glanced with despair at Running Elk, before she tried one last time to reason with the woman. "Jasmine, listen to me and hear what I say. You do not understand these people."

"And you do? You understand because you *like* their heathenish ways. You never tried to fit in with the white people. You resented my trying to civilize you. You *belong* here. I *do not!* And I won't give myself to them . . . no matter what!"

"Enough!" Running Elk commanded.

"Please?" Esther begged. "Just a minute more."

With a quirk of his eyebrow, Running Elk looked at Jasmine, alternately beseeching God to save her and hurling defiant insults at Tall Lance. Her behavior was incomprehensible to the war chief. He shrugged and shook his head, a look of contempt twisting his mouth.

"Jasmine, listen to me!" Esther waited for Jasmine to quiet again before she continued. "You will be staked to the ground and bound, hand and foot, and you will be helpless to save yourself."

At last, Esther's words broke through Jasmine's hysteria. Though her mouth remained open as if to loose another volley, her eyes cleared, and she studied the cold faces of the twenty warriors who rode up to investigate the commotion. When her appraisal reached Tall Lance, her eyes widened, and she recoiled under the pure fury radiating from him.

Recognizing the meaning in their looks, she paled, and her eyes darkened with the realization that Esther spoke the truth. "What must I do?" she asked frantically.

"You must do exactly as he says, and not make another sound. You have humiliated him in front of his friends and his leader, and it will be a while before he forgives you and looks with favor on you. To gain his respect again, you must bear your punishment with strength and make him proud that he selected you. Otherwise—" Esther's voice trailed away, but there was no mistaking her implication.

"I do not *want* his favor," Jasmine hissed, "and I do not care if he respects me or is proud of me. That's the silliest thing I ever heard—wanting a heathen savage to be *proud* of me. I did not ask him to take me, and I'll make him sorrier every day he keeps me." She sneered at Esther. "I have no intention of surrendering . . . like you!"

Esther's shoulders sagged. "Jasmine, you are a fool. You have seen women who've returned from captivity. They did not come back toothless, scarred, mindless

crones for no reason. Do you want to be like them?"
Esther looked at Tall Lance, growing impatient for their
conversation to end, running his bow across the palm of
his hand, and glaring at Jasmine from beneath hooded
eyes.

Jasmine turned wild eyes on Esther, then slumped in
defeat, her shoulders rounded and her head drooping on
her chest.

Tall Lance scowled at Jasmine for a minute more,
slung his bow over his shoulder, and sprang into the
saddle behind her. He dug his heels into his pony's ribs
and the two of them took off, leaving a trail of dust as
they streaked over the prairie.

"I hope she has the good sense to listen to you,"
Running Elk said softly and urged his horse forward to
join the rest of the warriors as they moved on. "She is a
fortunate woman to have you for a friend."

In silence they rode swiftly toward the cool shade of
pecan and sycamore trees clustered along the river. At
first glance, the tree-sheltered thicket on the bank
seemed empty, filled only with an eerie silence. Then
from the deep shadows, two boys of about fifteen
emerged, leading a string of spirited ponies. So well
concealed were the horses that a sharp whinny was the
only clue that anything was there. Strong hands worked
with practiced precision to remove the leather surcingles
binding the saddles to the weary ponies and transfer them
to fresh animals.

The goods stolen in the Comanche raids on settlers and
wagon trains were packed and padded to muffle any
noise and lashed to pack animals hidden in the thicket.

Out of the shadows stepped the warrior holding

Esther's Bible and herb chest. "Do you want me to carry these things all the way?" he asked Running Elk.

Running Elk looked at Esther and pointed to a heavy leather pouch hanging like a large brown scab on the side of one of the pack horses. She nodded and watched as the Indian gently lowered her precious items into the pouch.

A sharp, short shriek bit at the air . . . then silence. Esther's heart leaped in her chest. Jasmine! What was Tall Lance doing to her now?

Running Elk slipped over the rump of the sweat-stained black horse and began untying Esther's chafed ankles. She sat mute, making herself as unobtrusive as possible. She understood only too well that her survival depended on her behavior in these first few days. *Lord, please let Your Spirit be with me. Enfold me in Your loving arms. Help me bear with dignity what I must.*

As she finished praying, Brook Savage's face rose unbidden in her mind's eye. A sob caught in her throat. What would he think when he learned of her capture? Would he come after her? Would he even care? There was no reason he should risk his life on so dangerous a mission. After all, they scarcely knew one another. While she had lost her heart to him, they had spoken no words beyond polite conversation. He was bound in no way to her. But he had promised, and she held that promise in her heart like a talisman.

Running Elk pulled Esther down from the horse, jerking her back to reality. "Go," he said and pointed to a thick clump of bushes. Understanding that he was granting her privacy to tend to her personal needs, she managed a thin smile of gratitude and hurried off. In the copse, she came upon Jasmine sprawled on the ground.

Esther paused and regarded the struggling woman. "Jasmine, you are most foolish. You will live to regret your folly if you do not soon cooperate."

Raising her head and fixing Esther with an icy stare, Jasmine croaked through her tortured throat, "At least, I am a moral Christian woman, and I will go to my grave knowing I fought with my last breath to preserve my virtue . . . not like someone else I know." Her lips tightened. "And to think I believed the story you told about your previous captivity."

Esther sighed and disappeared into the privacy of the brush. Poor, stupid Jasmine. Esther prayed she would not have to be present when Tall Lance lost his patience completely.

When Esther returned, Running Elk helped her onto a different horse, a mean-tempered roan whose immediate goal was to take a healthy nip from the nearest person. A young boy jerked the big head down and held the reins tightly while Running Elk retied the lariat around Esther's raw ankles.

Another of the boys brought a rounded leather pouch that looked like the stomach of some large animal, not dissimilar to the one in which Esther's chest and Bible were stored. This one, filled with water, sloshed as he offered it to Running Elk. Accepting the vessel, the war chief balanced it lightly in his hands, toyed with it as though denying his great thirst. Then, before he drank, he looked hard at her.

For the first time since he had hoisted her onto the horse back at the wagon camp, she looked directly into his eyes. They were black bottomless pits registering no emotion. She kept her own expression neutral. She would not let him know of her great thirst, would not give water a thought. Would, in fact, watch with disinterest as he took long, gulping swallows.

How strange to be thinking like an Indian again. It all came back so easily. Perhaps Jasmine was right. All her efforts at civilizing Esther had merely laid a veneer over the real person, the Indian person underneath.

Something softened in Running Elk's eyes. Did she read admiration there? Finished, he raised the pouch to her lips. Avoiding his eyes, Esther took a small amount of the precious liquid, then returned the pouch to him.

Tall Lance walked over and Running Elk passed on the water pouch, his gaze never leaving Esther's face.

Tall Lance drank deeply, making sure he stood where Jasmine would see him. A longing look compressed her features, and she ran a dry tongue over cracked, bleeding lips. Having slaked his thirst, Tall Lance knelt as if to give Jasmine a drink. She raised her head to receive it, but when her mouth was but inches from the pouch, Tall Lance slowly poured her share on the ground, letting a tiny stream of water trickle into a muddy stain just out of her reach.

Jasmine stared in disbelief, then lowered her head into the dust and whimpered.

The Indians divided into small groups, each party taking a share of the spoils. In short order they were all mounted and riding off in different directions.

Here, Running Elk and Tall Lance separated, with Running Elk and Esther heading northwest toward the headwaters of the Arkansas River. Through the late afternoon hours and into the sunset, they rode, giving Esther reason to regret the fact that the eastern Indians with whom she had lived did not have horses, for she was not a skilled rider and was forced to grip the pommel with whitened fingers as the great beast surged over washes and hummocks. With each flying leap, she gave thanks that, at least, she was securely tied to the horse and braced by Running Elk's strong arm.

By the time darkness fell, Esther's only thoughts were concentrated on the rhythmic motion and unending pounding of the horses and the pain wracking her body. Clamped to the war chief's chest, she was drenched in sweat and bore the brunt of wind and sun as well, her face burned raw from the abuse.

They did not stop again, and Esther decided no mortal, man nor horse, could run like this for hours over the broiling prairie. Yet on they galloped. To save their mounts, the Indians alternated the pace from a lope to a fast walk, from a canter to a bouncing trot. Esther felt bruised, inside and out.

As the sky darkened, a brilliant moon rose in front of them, spilling light and shadows over the rounded hills and into the valleys. The sea of grass, green in the daylight, became a silver sea, shimmering in the press of the wind rippling through it. Variegated night hawks, silhouetted against the bright face of the moon, swooped and darted through the sky. In the distance, a wolf howled a lone mournful plea, and Esther's skin crawled.

Somewhere in the night, they met Tall Lance. Jasmine rode behind him, her hands unbound and her mouth free of a gag for once. She kept her balance by clutching the saddle. She traveled with her eyes closed, seemingly unaware of her surroundings.

There had been no sound from Jasmine since Tall

Lance rejoined Running Elk. Perhaps she had decided to stop fighting and live.

To block out the endless bobbing sameness of the land they crossed, Esther followed Jasmine's lead and closed her eyes. She rode unseeing, thinking of Savage, remembering each detail of his face, each moment of their time together.

If he had done as promised, he would have returned to the wagon train by now and discovered her gone. She prayed he would come soon.

eight

"We'll camp here and get a little shut-eye," Sergeant Haskell announced as Savage swung back into his saddle after concluding his tracking.

Savage whipped around and faced him. "*You* say! And *I* say we're riding after those wagons. Now!" He lashed the horse's rump with the reins.

Haskell's hand shot out and grabbed the bridle of Savage's horse, jerking it around. "The Indian pony tracks went off in the opposite direction from the wagon tracks," he said, his voice cold and shockingly forceful. "If they did circle back and attack the wagons, there ain't one thing we can do for 'em now." The bright moonlight cast few shadows, and he studied Savage carefully. "I do not know what's eatin' you, but do not take it out on these men. They rode a full patrol, then with only a break for fresh horses, they followed you out on this trek. It's after midnight. They've been in the saddle over eighteen hours and done precious little complainin' about it." Haskell swung his leg over the cantell of his saddle and stepped to the ground. "You can do what you like, Savage, but the rest of us are bivouackin' here tonight."

Savage opened his mouth to blast Haskell as a cowardly has-been, finishing out his army time pandering to a washed-up colonel. But something had changed in the sergeant. His jaw was set like granite and a defiant look sparked in his eyes.

Haskell raised his hand for silence, and Savage slowly closed his lips over the biting words he had ready.

· In that unfamiliar commanding voice, the sergeant continued, "In the mornin', after a good breakfast, we'll track your wagon train."

In his heart, Savage knew Haskell was right. He had been in the saddle even longer than the troops. Not normally a rash man, Savage usually did not rush into danger until he sized up all sides of the situation. Tonight, he had to admit to being overly tired. And that fact, coupled with his emotional involvement—a factor he had not reckoned with until this moment—added up to poor judgment.

Relenting, Savage gave Haskell a curt nod. "Take care of 'em, then," he snapped and rode across the trampled ground and into the thicket where he and Esther had talked in the early afternoon. Had it been only twelve hours since he sat here holding her hand? He looked at a spot, still matted from a sleeping pallet, bathed now in the Comanche moonlight, and a rush of pure fury at his helplessness pressed against his temples. *Savage, get hold of yourself. You won't be any use to her like this.*

Bone weary, he eased out of the saddle and tethered his horse at the foot of the giant old cottonwood he had leaned against when he came up from the river to find Esther. Spreading a blanket on the spot where they had sat, he stretched out and let her face drift into his mind, let the soft night wind carry her scent to him—a mixture of herbs and roses—heard the softness of her voice, husky and low, as she told him her story. He could listen to her talk for the rest of his life and never grow tired of so musical a sound. He wondered what her laugh would be like, guessed she had had little to laugh about, and that it would be a long time before he heard that sound . . . if ever.

The thought of those prancing Indian ponies stirred

through his mind, and he balled his hands into fists. He could not seem to put to rest the feeling that Esther had been taken captive. Rolling on his side, Savage tried to sleep, but her face remained before him. He saw muddy tears streaking her pale cheeks, and her long golden hair streaming out around her, matted with dirt and twigs. In his imagination, she lay limp, sprawled like a child's doll, against the trunk of a tree. The scene grew inside him until it became so real that cold sweat beaded on his forehead and his stomach grew queasy.

Levering himself up onto his elbow, thinking to mount and ride, he raked icy fingers through the tangle of sweat-dampened hair and recognized the futility of trying to follow a trail even in such bright moonlight. If the Comanche had taken Esther, and not circled to attack the wagon train, they could have ridden an incredible distance today, removing themselves as far as possible from the soldiers. Savage pounded his frustration into the ground with his fist. Grief would accomplish nothing.

Slowly he lay back down, resigning himself to the fact that he could not act until morning. He laced his fingers behind his head and stared up at the moon, transformed into a backlight behind the fluttering leaves of the trees silhouetted against it. Unable to sleep, he relived every second of the time with Esther, fixing the tiniest detail firmly in his heart and mind. Sometime toward morning, he acknowledged that he loved her and would devote the rest of his life to her.

At first light, Savage pulled himself upright, shook his head to clear it, and gazed for a brief moment at the small fire crackling in the pit used by the wagon people. Drowsy soldiers were dragging still-weary bodies out of bed and down to the river. Haskell, appearing amazingly fit and already dressed in a uniform that looked like it had just been freshly pressed, stood with his hands on his hips surveying the scene. "All right, you lazy sons of proud mothers," he bawled in the tough voice sergeants seemed born with, "get your blankets stashed and mount up. You can breakfast on biscuits and jerky while you ride."

A chorused groan rose from the shapeless, blanket-covered mounds, still trying to catch one last wink of sleep.

Savage rolled up onto his feet and moved with silent steps to untie his horse. Leading him to the river to drink and then up to where Haskell was putting out the cooking fire, Savage growled, "You finally ready to break camp?"

"In a minute" was the infuriating reply.

Savage heard the sizzle of water as it hit the flames, and every nerve snapped. "You also planning to sweep and dust before you leave?" he roared.

With the patient look reserved for recalcitrant children, the sergeant said calmly, "Perhaps, Mr. Savage, you would like to leave the fire burnin' so it can set the prairie ablaze."

Blast! The man was right, but Savage found his cocksureness almost beyond enduring this morning. Not bothering to reply, Savage swung into the saddle and settled himself.

Haskell gave the signal and waited as the line of soldiers moved slowly out along the tracks left by the wagon train as it rolled north.

Savage's horse danced in its eagerness to be gone and Savage shared the same eagerness. "Haskell," he said as he rode up next to the sergeant, "are you ready to ride, or take a Sunday canter through the park?"

Haskell looked straight ahead. "I shall proceed at a sensible pace. If that do not meet with your approval, maybe you should ride ahead. When your horse drops dead from abuse, you'll make excellent time walkin'."

Savage hesitated, looking up along the trail cut through the waving prairie grass, the trail made by the Comanches. Esther's voice seemed to call to him. He even went so far as to allow the horse a few steps in that direction, then bowing to logic, he laid the reins against the sturdy animal's neck and turned him in the direction the troops were taking.

Before he rode away, however, Savage looked again at the berry bushes and the blooming nut trees and imagined Esther sitting on the edge of a clear stream, dangling long firm legs in the cool water, letting the wind toy with the cornsilk-colored cascade rippling down her back. He felt the soft strands running through his fingers, tried to imagine her full soft lips on his, heard her voice as it murmured in harmony with the water, saw her gentle smile as she drew the cold knot of grief and revenge from his heart and filled the spot with warmth and love.

Savage, you poor lost soul, dreaming such things about a woman you've scarcely met!

Nevertheless, his feelings were real and would not be denied. He could not ride at such a pace as Haskell set. Shouting a farewell to the troops, he bent over Smoke and gouged the gelding with spurs. Not used to such treatment from Savage, the startled animal leaped into a gallop past the slow-moving line of soldiers.

Savage reset his hat low on his forehead and clenched his jaw. If something had happened to that wagon train and his woman had been hurt, Savage promised himself he would ride back to the fort as if all the demons of hell were after him and gut that mealy-mouthed coward of a regulation colonel!

He rode hard, covering the miles with little awareness, the image of Esther in need, the force driving him on. Having lost all sense of time, he was startled when a wisp of smoke signaled some kind of action just over the next rise. Crouching low over the sorrel's back, he topped the crest of the small hill and came upon the wagon train, stopped for their nooning near a grove of cottonwoods.

Savage lost no time in making camp, searching out the one face that had filled all his dreams. But it was Enoch Fisher's craggy features he saw first after he had dismounted. And in the grim set of the wagon master's shaggy white head, he read the message of defeat.

"She's gone, lad. Warn't nothin' I could do."

A deep pulsing fury replaced the hope of the last hours. The fury was self-directed. Against Savage's better judgment and all his instincts, he had let Haskell talk him into camping for the night. If he had ridden on as he had wanted, he could have reached Esther this morning. The thought seared his soul, and he slammed his gloved fist against the wagon box, trying to relieve the tension twisting his insides.

Now a single thought consumed him like a raging prairie fire: He must find Esther and bring her back before any serious harm befell her.

"I'm riding," he said shortly, whirling to remount Smoke and be off.

But Enoch put a restraining hand on Smoke's bridle. "One man against an army of Comanche on the warpath? Do not do it, boy. Wait for the Army. Judgin' by their dust," he said, eyeing the southern horizon, "they'll be along in another ten minutes or so."

Savage looked, then scowled fiercely. "Can't wait."

Enoch thrust a mug of hot coffee at Savage. "Can't afford not to. Take a few minutes, eat, and wait for reinforcements. Gather your strength, boy. Do not try to go it alone."

Knowing Enoch was right, Savage permitted himself to be talked into waiting and swung down out of the saddle. He accepted the coffee and walked over into the shade of a tall wagon to sip the potent brew.

Was he getting soft in his old age? Allowing himself to be delayed when he knew he should be riding was not like him, and Savage pondered this with some uneasiness as he waited for the troops to arrive.

He did not have long to wait. Haskell, leading the line, cantered up in front of Savage and dismounted. "What did you find out?"

Pitching the dregs of coffee into the dust, Savage tossed the cup into the back of the wagon and quickly recounted the story of Esther and Jasmine.

When he finished, Haskell exclaimed, "Well, I'll be! You've had a hunch all along, ain't you?"

Savage nodded.

"What are you goin' to do?"

"Go after them, of course."

"By yourself?"

"Do I have a choice? You going to let me have some men?"

Haskell fidgeted with his reins and looked down where the toe of his boot scooped the dust into little mounds. "I'd like to let 'em go, I really would. If it was up to me, there'd be no question. But you know our orders as well as I do. No ridin' after Indians without the colonel's permission. And he ain't likely to give any such command."

"Then I'm just wasting more time." Savage moved away to water his horse and reset the saddle.

Before they could talk more, Enoch came up to greet Haskell. "Mighty comfortin' to have you and your men along." He paused and cast an anxious eye at Savage.

"Unless, of course, you're plannin' on givin' that boy a hand."

Haskell shook his head. "Can't. Orders are to escort you folks up to the Oregon Trail, then head back to the fort. Boys would like a chance for a little action, but none of 'em is hankerin' to be court-martialed as a reward for a few scalps."

Pastor Waite, looking even more wraithlike than usual, brought a sack of food and handed it to Savage. "It's not much, but then I thought you'd be wanting to travel light."

"Much obliged," Savage said as he tied the bundle to his saddle.

Enoch stuck out a meaty paw. "Good huntin', son."

Savage took the old man's hand, wondering for an instant if either of them would be alive to see the colors of fall.

"Anything you can do to bring Sister Waite and Esther back to us will not go unrewarded," the pastor promised.

Savage nodded. Then, swinging into the saddle, he touched the brim of his hat with his fingers in a quick salute, and nudged his pony into a canter toward the northwest.

Savage did not know when he had been this tired. But worse than his weariness was the feeling of emptiness. Just when his life had started to have meaning again, everything had been swept away. It had been a long time, but the urge to pray edged in around the corners of his mind. However, when he tried, he could not find the words and the sense of loss turned icy.

Savage, you know better than to keep thinking this way. Can't find your woman unless you get hold of yourself. Being a practical man, he forced Esther from his mind. Torturing himself would accomplish nothing. Her rescue, which would motivate his every act from now on, was going to take time, maybe a lot of time—weeks, months, maybe even years. A man alone was going to have to plan carefully, take his time, do nothing rash.

The moment for surprise was long gone, the need to hurry over. Savage cut across the open rolling prairie in a straight line, hoping to intercept the trail of the Comanche. They should be riding north, but with a war brewing, it was hard to tell what they would do.

The sun was casting shadows on the trail when he heard galloping hooves coming up behind him. Quickly, he looked for shelter. There was not a tree or rock anywhere. He was caught in the open with no place to hide, and he would have to take his licks if he could not talk his way out of trouble.

He pulled up and turned to face the approaching horseman, leaving his hands spread at his sides in full view. "Well, I'll be—" Savage said under his breath as he watched the uniformed figure riding toward him.

When he was close enough to hear, Savage shouted, "Haskell, you lost or you out recruiting scouts?"

A wide grin split Haskell's sunburned face as he drew to a halt. "Got to thinkin' as I was ridin' along beside that wagon train that I ain't had this much fun in years, ever since I started takin' the safe route. Do not have no family. Not a soul in this world cares whether I live or die but me. Kept thinkin' about going back to that office and six more months of doin' reports from the yellow-bellied colonel. Did not hardly seem the way to close out a long and honorable career." He gave Savage a sheepish grin. "I'd like to ride along, if you'll have me."

"But what about your pension and all you've worked for? This little sortie could take more'n six months. They'll get you for desertion and you'll be left high and dry."

"Naw, not with my record. Put the troops under a leathery old corporal who's been busted from sergeant more times that he can remember. He'll tell the colonel I went out to scout the country and did not come back. He can only presume I got captured, but with orders not to chase the Indians, was not a thing he could do for me. Now that ain't a lie." He laid the reins in a show of turning his horse around. "Of course, if you do not want me along—"

Savage reached out and clapped the man on the back. "You sure put on a good show back at the fort, Haskell. Never would have guessed desertion lay black and dark in your heart. Sure, I want you. Two can do a lot more than one and you know it."

Haskell removed his hat and, using the sleeve of his once-spotless uniform, wiped the stream of sweat seeping down in front of his ears. "Well, if you're ready, I am," he said. "Let's go get me some Comanches, and you a wife."

Savage looked at Haskell from beneath the low brim of his hat. "Who said anything about a wife?"

Haskell gave a hard chuckle. "Boy, you been lookin' like a moon-eyed hound dog ever since we got back to where that wagon train was supposed to be. Nothin' brings that out in a man but a woman."

Savage did not bother to deny Haskell's words. Suddenly, the air seemed clearer, the wind fresher. A brisk gust rippled the brim of his soft hat as he turned back to the east. He bent his head, and glanced at Haskell. The big man was looking at him, a grin crinkling his face.

"So, you want to help me get my woman back, let's ride." Savage urged his pony into a brisk canter and the two men, heads high, set their course.

nine

Before dawn, on the morning of the third day of her capture, Esther opened her eyes. The aroma of stolen coffee brewing in a large copper kettle wafted over to her, and she looked with hunger-widened eyes at fileted buffalo steaks draped from long, sharpened sticks planted around the cookfire. The sizzle of the juices dripping into the flames and the rich aroma of the roasting meat made her mouth water and knotted her empty stomach.

Crouched on his haunches before the fire, Running Elk chomped on hunks of the steak, wiping the grease on his leggings and talking in low, guttural tones with some of his men.

As he visited, he reached out casually with the tip of his knife and nursed an especially delicious-looking piece of meat. When he was satisfied that it was done, he eased the strip from its skewer, rose unobtrusively, and walked away from the circle, past where Esther lay. He paid her no heed, but just before he disappeared into the trees, she heard a plop in the leaves above her head.

Pretending to be asleep, she rolled over onto her stomach. Resting her head on her chin, Esther found herself staring at the succulent meat. Trembling fingers darted out, grasped it, and dropped it just as fast. She licked the juices from her burning fingertips, then judiciously blew on the meat to cool it.

Thank you, God, for touching Running Elk's heart, she prayed, and restrained herself from wolfing down the first food she had had in three days, so tender that she tore it to bite-sized pieces with her fingers. Exercising great restraint, she forced herself to chew each bite thoroughly, lingering over the tasty meal.

Finished at last, she pushed herself into a sitting position and wiped the last traces of grease on the tattered remnants of her skirt. Wishing fervently for water, both to drink and to wash in, she scanned the busy camp. Here, without their women to do the menial tasks, the men, with surprising efficiency, had taken over the preparing of the meat from their hunt and the cooking of it. They had also set up and struck the camp with practiced ease, each seeming to have an appointed task in the overall scheme.

Suddenly, a thin, croaking wail disturbed the orderly clamor of preparations to leave. Jasmine, her haunted, red-rimmed eyes sunk deep in their sockets, staggered out of the trees across the clearing. She walked with shuffling steps, jerked along by the leather cord Tall Lance still kept around her throat. As they passed the men packing the last of the supplies and equipment, the laughing warriors stopped their work and formed an aisle.

Esther, distressed but helpless, shook her head at Jasmine's plight and offered a brief prayer for the poor woman. If only they would soon arrive at the main camp, perhaps Esther would be permitted to talk with her and offer her some hope. Tall Lance must care greatly for her not to have tortured her to death before now. She must make Jasmine understand that.

Weaving his way through the milling crowd, Running Elk crossed the clearing, a head taller than all the others. Approaching Esther, he hunkered down before Esther. He had washed off the war paint, revealing the sharp angles of high cheekbones and a finely chiseled nose. His intelligent eyes, spread wide apart, looked at her with cold indifference as he worked at the knots around her blood-scabbed ankles.

Determined not to let him intimidate her, she signed, "Thank you for the food," and forced cracked lips into a crooked smile.

For a brief moment the cold mask dropped from his face, and the warm glow in his dark eyes stunned Esther. She went rigid. Why had it failed to occur to her before that he had captured her to make her his wife? The signs were now most obvious, particularly when she recalled that the warriors had ridden away peacefully and made no attack on the wagon train.

But then perhaps she should not condemn herself, Esther thought. No doubt in these past three days, her discernment had suffered in her preoccupation with Jasmine's treatment and her own desire to spare herself most of the abuse normally rained on white captives.

The last knot slipped loose, freeing her feet. Fierce needles of pain raced up her cold, bloodless legs, and she almost wished for a return of the numbness.

Slowly, Running Elk withdrew his scalping knife from the leather sheath strapped to his thigh.

Esther held her breath and stared, trancelike, at the thin blade glittering in the first rays of morning sun.

He placed the flat of the knife against her lips. Then, moving the blade to the hollow beneath her right ear, he lay the fine tip against her skin and drew it skillfully in a light line under her chin, and up to her other ear. There he held it, gave a quick twist, just enough to draw blood, and with a trembling hand, returned the red-tipped instrument to its sheath.

"If you do not try to run away, I will leave you untied," he said, his voice unusually husky.

His meaning was clear. He did not want to, but he would kill her if she forced him. Esther shrank back, nodding her understanding.

Suddenly Esther was aware that the bustle of the busy camp had subsided. She looked past Running Elk, observing that most of the warriors had paused to watch their chief with his prisoner. Glancing at their stern countenances, he gave a deep sigh and reached into his bag, bringing out a noose similar to the one Tall Lance used to lead Jasmine about. Slipping it over Esther's head and tightening it around her neck, he stood and jerked her to her feet by the cord, sending a shower of stars behind her eyes. Grim lines altering his handsome features, he stalked away and Esther, staggering and stumbling on her still numb lumps of feet, trailed meekly along behind him.

Seeing her thus secured, the men finished packing away the makings of the overnight camp and strolled off to claim their horses.

While Running Elk held her neck thong loosely in his hand, she followed him in the direction of the staked horses and stared at his well-muscled back, rigid and forbidding. She understood that Running Elk had to test her. If she were not strong and brave, worthy to be the wife of a powerful war chief, he must know it now. Still, watching the slack of the line around her neck nearly drag the ground, she knew he would permit only the most necessary trials to be inflicted on her. She lifted her head resolutely and pledged to bring no shame to him.

She knew she was lucky to have been captured by one

such as Running Elk since she would spend her life as an Indian. For she did not want to return to the white world after a second season of bondage to suffer greater humiliation and rejection than she had experienced the first time. There would be no other as understanding as Pastor Waite.

Though she had heard that people in the West were more understanding, she did not believe it. People were people wherever they lived, and those who had not experienced the trials of captivity lacked any real sympathy for the captive.

No, Running Elk, she vowed silently. *I will not try to escape.* Unless a miracle occurred, this man would likely be her husband for the rest of her days on this earth, and she would do well to please him.

Then, deliberately, she conjured the image of Savage's face, tracing his every feature mentally, feeling his presence strong around her. As she concentrated on the brilliant morning star just above the horizon, it seemed to act as a bond linking the two of them together. With the coming of dawn, slowly the image of his face slipped, blurred, and disappeared as though he had stopped thinking of her.

Esther sighed. It was probably just as well. It was not wise to dwell on an impossible dream, and so she forced all thought of him away.

When she and Running Elk arrived at the thicket where the horses milled about, a young boy handed him the reins to two fine-looking ponies already saddled. The war chief nodded his acceptance of the horses. Turning to Esther, his face now an immobile mask, he gave her the reins to a sorrel dancing in a circle around them.

With a dignified tip of her head, Esther nodded her thanks and accepted the lines. She decided at that moment that, if she was to ride alone, she would not be tethered to Running Elk. Since the Indians admired independence in their women, she hoped this was the proper time to demonstrate hers. Keeping her eyes fixed on him, she reached up with deliberation and slipped the noose from her neck and handed it to him. Her fingers trembled slightly at the daring of her act, but she pushed down the thoughts of possible consequences if she proved to be wrong. She thought she saw a twitch of amusement at the corners of the Elk's mouth, but it was so fleeting she could not be sure.

Her heart pounding erratically as she walked around to the right side of the horse, Esther mounted the powerful sorrel with some expertise gained over the past three grueling days. Seeing she was safely in the saddle, Running Elk leaped onto his stunning black stallion, now brushed and shining, and galloped to the head of the line of warriors.

Attempting to imitate his manner of communicating with a horse, Esther pressed her knees into its ribs, and the pony sprang forward, nearly unseating her. Until today she had been tied to the saddle, and only now could she appreciate the safety that had afforded. But by clasping the pommel in a death grip, Esther managed to arrive in line behind Running Elk without losing her seat.

With the freedom of her own horse, she should have enjoyed the day, but as they rode away from the camp, she felt eyes on her, unfriendly eyes that over the next hours grew increasingly hostile. Trying not to appear obvious, she searched the group, but no one seemed to be paying her the slightest attention.

Tall Lance rode at the rear of the group with Jasmine in front of him, hands bound to the pommel, body so slumped her head rested nearly on the horse's neck. Tall Lance looked straight ahead, his face an angry mask, the ferocity of his feelings accented by the white scar twisting across his left cheek and into the corner of his mouth. Over the days since the women's capture, Tall Lance had changed. His eyes had taken on a hard glitter. Apparently Jasmine brought out the violence in him and kept it boiling. Esther shuddered when she thought of the woman's future.

The sun crawled high into the sky, then having reached its zenith, began the hot descent toward evening. The hours of the afternoon blended into one another and would have been as monotonous as the other days had it not been for the crawling feeling running along her back. To escape, she urged her pony into a canter and rode up beside Running Elk.

Surprise flickered over his face and he stared at her with an intensity she found unsettling. She lowered her eyes, only to have him reach over and roughly tip her chin up and around, forcing her to look at him. It took a moment to register that he wanted to see her eyes. She had forgotten the fascination her brilliant azure eyes held for an Indian. Now, it seemed, they drew Running Elk like a magnet, and she watched desire for her flame in his face.

Esther wanted desperately to turn away, but knew she dared not until he chose to dismiss her. He took her hand, and it was at that instant that she felt a bolt of loathing strike her as if it were a physical blow. She winced, and he dropped her hand.

Realizing she had offended him, she paled and signed quickly, "I apologize. I find your hand comforting, the more so because someone behind is sending hate-filled thoughts to me. I cannot see who it is, but I feel the anger."

Running Elk did not answer at once, in fact, rode for some time as though he had not heard. Then he asked, "Do you still feel it?"

Esther nodded.

"We will drop back a little at a time until you are no longer aware of the feeling. It will not be hard to tell who it is." He slowed and Esther followed his lead, letting those in back ride past. The closer to the rear they moved, the more intense the feelings became until Esther expected at any minute to be stabbed or shot. Whirling about, she found herself looking directly into Tall Lance's black, glittering eyes, eyes that continued to discharge his venom at her, making no attempt at concealment.

There was no way she could tell Running Elk of her discovery. He and Tall Lance had ridden side by side until today, when Jasmine had forced Tall Lance to retreat to a place of low esteem. Perhaps he hated Esther, she guessed, because she brought no such shame to Running Elk.

Finally, she and the chief rode at the back behind Tall Lance. Once more, Running Elk looked to her, awaiting confirmation, but she shrugged and signed, "I cannot be sure."

He nodded and sent his pony racing forward. Esther joined him, glad to be in front again, out of the dust. Looking back from time to time, she always found Tall Lance staring at her with his bead-black eyes.

In the late evening, just as the last light turned the sky

pearly, they returned to the camp they had left that morning. The Comanche must feel danger, Esther decided, and were splitting into small groups, making many tracks, circling, creating an impossible trail to follow. Tonight many fewer people sought shelter in the woods. There was no fire and no visiting. While their captives huddled in miserable heaps, the warriors ate cold meat and loudly slurped their fill of water. Running Elk tied Esther securely, feet and hands, and gave her nothing.

On this night, Esther lay staring up at the stars flickering like tiny candles in the inky blackness of the sky, still moonless. In spite of her vow, she thought of Savage. She knew it was a futile and needless torture, but she drew a measure of comfort from remembering his soft gray eyes as they studied her face, the notch in his chin he rubbed when he was thinking, his deep rumble of a voice that gentled when he spoke her name. He seemed so near, as though the stars were his eyes. Then, once more, her awareness of him slipped away.

She huddled into the leaf mold that made her bed and shivered with the cool breeze blowing across her uncovered body. Her teeth grated on the dust and the insides of her eyelids scratched like fine sandpaper.

Mounds of warm buffalo robes scattered around the clearing told where the men slept, though a few of the warriors were restless and wandered to the edge of the trees to gaze out over the undulating prairie, silvery-white under the newly risen Comanche moon. Twice, Tall Lance rose, walked close to Esther, his look sending chills through her body as he passed by.

She lay listening to the night sounds. The distant howl of a wolf, the yipping of a lone coyote, the never-ending crickets sawing at the air, the eerie cry of the screech owl all conspired to overwhelm Esther with the hopelessness of escaping this hostile, featureless world. Besides the wild animals and snakes to keep her prisoner, hunger and thirst and slow death guarded her well. She bit her lip until she tasted blood. Tightly shutting her eyes and concentrating on Savage's face, she managed, for a few fanciful minutes, to create a measure of comfort and hope.

But always, invading her last conscious thoughts and stealing her small scrap of peace was the image of Tall Lance, spearing her with his black and fearsome gaze.

ten

The Comanche called the Colorado River, Talking Water River for good reason, Esther knew. Its rumble could be heard for miles before one could ride close enough to see into the great canyon beyond the high bluff. Racing, leaping rapids churned over the rock-strewn bed, making conversation impossible.

Today, the party rode for several miles along the north canyon edge overlooking the rich, narrow bottomlands. Late in the afternoon they stopped at an imposing pile of boulders, dismounted, and began riffling through their packs.

When the warriors pulled out their war gear, Esther's heart jumped at the sight. Were they going to attack a lonely cabin of defenseless people? Was there a settlement hidden away here in this wilderness? Though she had not seen the aftermath of a Comanche raid, she had heard of little else since leaving Independence.

Please, God. Do not let them raid and massacre helpless people, Esther silently prayed.

While the men dressed, pulling up their fancy beaded leggings heavy with fringe and tying them to breechclouts, Esther moved her horse to the outside of the trail. Here, though she was still close to Running Elk and in his line of vision, she could see into the valley.

The warriors painted themselves, then greased, rebraided their hair, and wrapped the heavy braids in strips of beautiful furs—otter, beaver, and ermine. Sliding their war shields carefully from their protective soft leather cases, the warriors shook and straightened the feathers rimming them. Running Elk tied up the black's tail as for war, and braided feathers and bells into his mane.

While everyone was thus occupied, Esther searched the valley frantically for signs of settlers. She determined that if necessary, she would scream a warning and keep screaming until her captor killed her. If she saved even one life, her death would not be futile.

As though reading Esther's mind, Running Elk halted in his battle preparations long enough to slip the noose around her neck and tie the other end to his wrist. He gave her a stern look, indicating that she was to follow and give no trouble. Even Jasmine had the good sense to remain silent.

In their war finery, the Comanche mounted their gaily decorated horses. The warriors, their bows and quivers strapped to their glistening backs and shields hanging from tough sinewy left arms, rode with streamers fluttering and lances held at the ready.

They rode along the river bluff westward into the setting sun until, in the afterglow just before dark, a settlement appeared. Not the white settlement Esther had expected, however, but hundreds of squat conical tents scattered among the cottonwoods, rising tall along the river bank.

A roaring fire in the center of the village sent tortured shadows writhing across the pale tan curves of the nearest lodges. Running Elk gave a long, howling cry that was picked up and echoed by his men. Below, hundred of throats took up the call until the low, wide canyon echoed with the sound.

War ponies raced over the edge of the cliff and plunged headlong down the steep night-darkened slope. Small avalanches of stones and dirt clattered and snapped as they rumbled to the bottom, reaching there only seconds before the riders.

Running Elk waited until all his men were down, then he plunged with equal fury over the edge. Esther, terror pumping through her, clamped her eyes shut and sent her pony over the edge. Concentrating on staying in the saddle and not pitching off head-first into the dense clumps of prickly pear cactus dotting the ground, she rode her way down.

The horses smelled home and, once her pony struck level ground, he reared, gave a sharp whinny, and joined the others in the race for the village. Arriving at the outermost tents, the warriors reined in the ponies and, with Running Elk back in the lead, paraded slowly and with solemn dignity through the narrow streets.

Not much different from a Delaware or Seneca homecoming, Esther thought, *except the Comanche make their entrance on horseback.*

Kin and friends surrounded the heroes, chanting and yelling their excitement and joy at a safe return for their men. A cluster of small boys fell in beside them, imitating the war whoops and waving their small bows and lances, duplicates of those the warriors carried.

Arriving at the huge bonfire that had been built in the center of the village, everyone dismounted and fell into the welcoming arms of loved ones. Running Elk hugged a withered old woman, her face wreathed with smiles. In the background stood a beautiful young woman, wearing an elaborately decorated green chamois dress. Her wide dark eyes were fixed only on Running Elk, her face aglow with her feelings. He paid her no mind except for a casual nod, but she continued to smile a genuine undimmed smile as though his scant attention was enough.

With shuttered eyes, Running Elk regarded Esther, still mounted on her horse. Roughly he jerked the line around her neck, pulled her from the horse, and sent her sprawling into the dust. Leaving her there, he walked away, abandoning her to the mob.

As the night stretched on, the celebration built in intensity. A blur of blankets, leather fringes, buffalo robes swirled around Esther.

Suddenly someone grabbed a hank of her hair and held it up for all to see. A knife flashed, and she felt a strand leave her scalp. Others wanting a lock of the golden hair reached out to snatch it, but she fought back, shrieking as fiercely as they.

Grabbing the first dark head of hair that came into view, she held on with the tenacity of a wolverine defending her newborn cub. Pulling and kicking with complete abandon, Esther was scarcely aware when everyone but the person she held captive backed away and grew silent and she found herself staring at leather leggings planted wide apart in front of her.

"Let her go," Running Elk ordered.

Slowly, Esther untwined her fingers from the hair she held and found herself looking into the lovely face of the green-robed woman. Running Elk jerked Esther to her feet, whirled her around, and gave her a vicious shove. The force propelled her down the street.

"Go!" he commanded and followed some distance behind.

Still clutching a handful of long black hair, Esther staggered along the dusty roadway past dark vacant lodges, their inhabitants silhouetted against the firelight.

What is he going to do with me? she agonized, her insides

knotting with dread.

Her heart pounding wildly and terror nearly blinding her, Esther stumbled on in the direction he had shoved her. As they passed each lodge, he gave her another push that staggered her and nearly sent her plunging to the ground. Finally, they arrived at a lodge in a quiet section of the village.

"Here!" Running Elk growled and threw aside a hide flap covering the door and called to someone inside.

"Makes Medicine, I have brought you a gift. I had to save the People from her. Star Flower was in danger of being scalped!" He looked down at the black hair Esther still clutched in her fist. "This one's name is Esther, and she makes good medicine. I watched her prepare herbs for the sick on the wagon train. She will be your legs and be much help to you."

"Thank you, Running Elk," came a low gentle voice from the darkness inside the lodge. "But are you sure you brought this child for my use?"

Peering inside, Esther recognized the bent little woman who had hobbled out to greet Running Elk upon his arrival. Now her broad, flat face wrinkled with smiles of delight.

Giving her full attention now to Esther, Makes Medicine's little black eyes examined her carefully. "When she is dressed, she will be beautiful. It is time you took a wife. You need sons." She circled Esther, squinting closely, not missing a single detail. "She make you *fine* sons . . . strong, tall."

Running Elk squirmed and shuffled his feet in the dust. "We shall see, little mother," he said without looking at Esther. "But until I decide what to do with her, I would like her to stay here and help you." He sent Esther a meaningful look. "She will give you no trouble."

Makes Medicine reached out talonlike fingers and clutched Esther's arm. "Yes, yes, I think she understands our ways. Right now, though, she looks weary. Leave her and go back to your celebrating. You have earned this night."

Running Elk gave Esther one final piercing look, a warning that she had no intention of ignoring, then strode off in the direction of the fire and clamor.

Guiding Esther inside the tent, Makes Medicine left her standing on the hard-packed dirt floor and scurried off toward a pile of buffalo robes. There, in the great untidy mound, she searched for something. The warm close air, heavy with a wild blend of odors, seemed to smother Esther and while she waited, she swallowed waves of nausea. She concentrated on giving grateful thanks for being spared more abuse, but nothing would stop the sudden swaying on aching battered legs, weak from lack of food. For a moment she feared she would faint. But this would surely anger Makes Medicine.

Esther wondered what her life would be like with Makes Medicine. Wondered how she would be treated, wondered if Star Flower was a wife to Running Elk, then decided she was not but would like to be. Wondered . . . a wave of heat swept over her, bile rose in her throat, and though she fought the inevitable, Esther's knees buckled. Slowly, she sank onto the floor, her mind hovering at the top of the tent. Then everything went black.

Sometime later, she was not sure just how long, Esther felt strong hands lift her and stretch her out on a soft bed. A warm cover dropped over her and she sighed. Tomorrow would come, but for now she could sleep, warm and comfortable. Gentle fingers stroked her hair back from her face, and she fluttered her eyes open for a second. Running Elk crouched next to her pallet, his attention fixed on something Makes Medicine was saying.

Esther relaxed, knowing she had nothing more to fear from the People. Running Elk would protect her.

Then, silently, in the doorway and unseen by Running Elk, Tall Lance appeared, his scarred face twisted into a cruel leer, and the look he pinned on Esther sent cold chills shuddering through her.

Yes, Running Elk would protect her from that which he could see, but he would never suspect Tall Lance, his friend and companion, of wishing her harm. The cold hard knot of fright returned to her stomach and, though Running Elk stayed by her side through the night, it was daybreak before Esther drifted off into a troubled sleep.

eleven

This morning began like every other morning since Esther's arrival in the Comanche village four months ago. Peering from under the warm buffalo robe, she watched the smoke from the cooking fire spiral upward to be sucked out through the hole fifteen feet above the floor. The thin leather tepee, a large cone shape, was staked over hard dirt still spiked with tough buffalo grass. Motes of dust filled the shaft of morning sunlight until it appeared as a solid object slanting in through the open door to spotlight the jumble of furs and buffalo robes on the two raised bedsteads against the far curved wall.

With the men still away hunting and raiding most of the time, there was a minimum amount of work for those left in camp. So they spent the long cool evening hours of September visiting, and even the children went to bed at no appointed hour. Because of this, the village awakened slowly to the day.

Now, the late morning sun seeped through the translucent walls and washed the heaped bags and bulging rawhide boxes with a warm, golden haze. Today, however, the camp churned with the clank of pots and talk. Esther threw back the robe and sat up, listening intently with her ear against the wall of the lodge. Word had just come that the men would be home this evening.

Quickly, she slipped into her moccasins and hurried outside. Bent over the big copper kettle Running Elk had brought as a gift when he gave her Esther, Makes Medicine looked up. "Good morning, daughter."

Esther smiled. "Good morning, Makes Medicine." She peered into the pot hanging on a tripod over the fire. "Why are you cooking out here?"

"You needed your sleep after helping Waving Grass get her baby here. Slow Walk says, without you, the child would not be alive."

Esther, still unaccustomed to such lavish praise, blushed, picked up a knife and began cutting the tops off a bunch of wild onions before she dropped the whole bulbs in the pot. The aroma curling in the air mixed with that of the hot coffee at the edge of the fire and reminded Esther how hungry she was. With Waving Grass only fourteen and small, it had been a long night and a difficult birth.

Finished with the onions, she took the flat wooden stir stick and fished out a piece of meat. While it cooled, she poured a cup of coffee, added some water to dilute the strong brew, and sipped it. "How else may I help?" she asked Makes Medicine.

Straightening, the old woman passed the back of one hand over her sweaty brow and with the other, made a fist and pushed a kink from her back. "You can tend to the sick today while I cook. I will not have you around much longer to do that for me."

Esther drew up sharply. "What do you mean?"

Makes Medicine looked carefully at her. "You do not know?"

Esther shook her head.

"Running Elk has been collecting a large number of horses to trade for you. He knows you are the finest woman in the tribe, and he must not insult you by offering me too few ponies. Rides Fast came this morning to tell us that Running Elk and the men are successful in their raids and have many horses." Makes Medicine smiled a toothless smile and smacked Esther across the rear in a show of affection. "He will take you from me now to be his wife."

Hoping her face did not betray her alarm, Esther absorbed the news like the kick of a mule in the pit of her stomach. With Running Elk away most of the summer, she had been safe and serene and almost happy here in the village, making herself useful and getting to know the Indian women and the old men who could no longer fight or hunt. Still, she had expected Savage to appear and take her away by now. Her mind raced with only half-formed plans for her escape.

"I am greatly honored, Makes Medicine," she said as calmly as she could manage. "When do you expect him to come with the horses?"

"The warriors will council tonight and maybe tomorrow night." The old woman paused and stared off across the valley. "I think he will come in three days. He is getting very anxious to take you from me."

"How do you know that?"

Makes Medicine's eyes widened and her mouth dropped open. "Do not you know he has much feeling for you . . . here?" She clasped her hands to her sagging bosom. "His eyes follow you everywhere."

Esther's face grew hot under Makes Medicine's scrutiny. "But does he not see Star Flower's eyes following him? She is the one he should be honoring with all those horses."

Giving the stew one last stir, Makes Medicine laid aside the stick and shuffled toward the lodge. "I agree." She turned her wizened face to Esther, nodding solemnly. "Star Flower has loved Running Elk since she was a little girl. There has never been another in her eyes. But a man cannot control his heart. You have taken his heart prisoner, and he is helpless."

"I have made no move to do that thing," Esther said, appalled that Running Elk's intentions toward her were the talk of the camp.

"Perhaps that is why he finds he cannot live without you. He is very handsome and powerful and all the maidens make eyes at him. But there is no thrill of the hunt in that. You give him nothing, and he craves you. That is the way of it." She shrugged matter-of-factly. "Do you feel no love at all for him?"

Would Makes Medicine talk among the women if Esther told her how she really felt? Running Elk had been very kind and gentle with her. Because the Comanche respected their women, he had never made an improper advance toward her. He had spent time teaching her the fine points of riding, hunting, and tracking. In the few days he had been in camp, they had had good times together. He had been particularly impressed when he learned of her years with other tribes and asked many questions. For all the good in him, Esther loved Running Elk like a brother.

But Savage was never far from her thoughts, and each day she grew more certain he was the man she must marry. Perhaps today was the day he would come for her. From habit, she stopped a moment and scanned the high bluffs. But there was nothing there but worn denim sky.

Holding back a sigh of longing, Esther looked into Makes Medicine's eager face and decided against confiding in her. "How could I not feel something in my heart for him? As you say, he is most wonderful."

The answer pleased Makes Medicine, for a wide smile wrinkled her old face and she chuckled happily as she hobbled back inside the lodge.

The sun was drifting past noon, when Esther set out for her

daily visit to Jasmine. She hurried across to the other side of the village, where Tall Lance lived with his three wives. Still some distance away, she could hear the commotion. Breaking into an easy run, she hurried in the direction of the ruckus.

Esther arrived to see Jasmine, a thick piece of kindling in one hand and a quirt in the other, encircled by neighboring women and children keeping a healthy distance. Inside the circle, Digs Much, one of Tall Lance's wives, was scrambling about in the dust on hands and knees, trying to escape Jasmine's flailing weapons.

Esther knew that Digs Much was selfish and lazy and not well liked by her neighbors. Now they gathered to make sport of her, laughing and shouting and placing wagers on the results of the fight. There had not been this much excitement in days, and even such an event as this was a welcome break in the monotony of their lives as they waited for the men to return.

Tall Lance's second wife, Whitewater, a much larger woman than Jasmine, stepped out of the crowd and wrenched the club from her hand. Throwing it far out of reach, Whitewater grabbed the quirt, but before she could land a blow, Jasmine spun and, spreading her long fingers like talons, struck at Whitewater's bulging eyes, while Digs Much set up a steady howl. The crowd cheered as the intensity of the fight increased.

With eyes wild and hair streaming down her back in a tangled mat, Jasmine hissed ominously, stooping to scoop up a handful of dust. Esther moved forward, crying out for the violence to cease. But the general uproar blotted up her words, and they went unnoticed.

When Whitewater approached Jasmine once more with the upraised quirt, Esther forced her way into the circle.

"Whitewater!" she shouted. "Put down that whip. You know Digs Much has been unfeeling and cruel to Jasmine ever since Tall Lance brought her here to help you. She is just trying to defend herself."

"The white slave has been no help!" Whitewater retorted. "She only causes trouble!"

Esther fixed a firm eye on Jasmine, who opened her fist and let the dirt sift through her fingers. Turning to Whitewater, Esther spoke quietly. "I agree with you. Jasmine has much to learn, but Tall Lance will be furious with you if he comes back and finds her disfigured and ugly. You know how he takes pleasure in her red hair."

Grudgingly, Whitewater tucked the quirt in the band of her skirt and stomped back to the river where she had been washing her cooking pots.

Digs Much scuttled into the lodge and, the show over, the neighbors, except for the wounded—those who had ventured too near Jasmine's weapons—went back to their preparations for the returning warriors.

Now the victims of the altercation gathered around Esther, pointing to their various cuts and bruises. As they passed by the still-prone Jasmine, each in turn planted a kick on her for inflicting the injury.

"If you will bring your herbs, I shall mix them and apply them for you," Esther said. And for the next few minutes, she ministered to their needs. Finally, however, she and Jasmine were alone.

The woman still lay sprawled in a heap in the dirt, a gaunt shadow of her former plump self. Dressed in scraps and patches gleaned from rags and leftover pieces of buckskin and sewn into a crazy-quilt pattern, Jasmine looked like a scarecrow. When the light breeze picked up her tattered skirt and flapped it against her thin body, Esther could see the cuts and bruises covering the woman's arms and legs, and her once ladylike hands were filthy and calloused.

The thick copper-colored hair she had always kept styled with such pride hung in matted ropes, greasy and snarled beyond the ability of a comb or brush to untangle. Esther knew that Jasmine bathed seldom and made every attempt to be personally repulsive, thinking to keep Tall Lance at a distance.

From her prone position, she watched Esther sink gracefully to the ground beside her. "You heard that the men are returning this evening?" Esther asked.

Jasmine did not reply, but picked up another handful of dust and let it sift through her fingers.

"Is that why you started beating Digs Much? In your heart was it Tall Lance you wished to hurt?"

Again Jasmine was mute, retreating into some safe corner of her mind.

But Esther persisted. "If you fear him so, why do not you try to please him for a change? He might even be gentle with you."

Still no reply.

"On the other hand, Makes Medicine says the men will sit at the council table much of tonight and tomorrow night as well. Tall Lance may not come home for some time yet." She watched Jasmine carefully, gauging the effect of her words. Encouraged by a flicker of response, Esther continued her monologue.

"You have suffered much, but let me tell you my story. The Lord blessed me when I was first captured by allowing me to be taken in by a family with a fine Christian woman as a slave. She talked with me about the Lord and let me speak

English as well as the language of the People. Then, when
the Seneca captured me from the Delaware, I was given to
the medicine woman of that tribe. She was also a Christian.
My faith has not been tested under such terrible circumstances—" She paused. "You see, you are really quite strong
to have endured so much without breaking." Esther
breathed a quick prayer for direction. Only the eyes of the
Lord could see into Jasmine's twisted mind, her wounded
spirit, and could guide Esther's words. "God has placed a
strength within you that you have not begun to tap."

Again she waited for a sign that Jasmine was receiving her
challenge before going on. "If I did not believe that, Jasmine,
I would not be sharing with you now. Listen to me—" She
paused once more, dropping her voice lest a passerby might
overhear them. "There is a man . . . a good man . . . who is
searching for us. There is a very good chance that we will be
rescued soon. But even if we are not, you must not give up.
God is here with us. All you have to do is trust Him. He
understands what you are suffering better than anyone else,
and He will not hold anything you have done against you.
But you will surely lose your mind and desire to live if you
dwell on your circumstances—"

Jasmine's face lost a little of its despair, and a tear formed,
spilling down her cheek and mixing with the dirt to leave a
tell-tale track down her cheek.

"Jasmine," Esther leaned forward and whispered in her
ear, "I have a plan . . . a plan to escape—"

This time Jasmine pulled herself into a sitting position and
pinned Esther with a searching look. "Escape?" she croaked.

"Hush now!" Esther put a warning finger to her lips.
"Someone may hear us. But if you'll listen, I'll tell you as
much as I can." Satisfied that Jasmine was alert now, she

sketched the barest outline of the proposed getaway, keeping it simple so the woman could follow.

"I have packed food for both of us," she went on. "I'll come for you tonight . . . while the entire village is celebrating the warriors' return. We can be well away from here by the time anyone misses us. Do you understand?"

"Y—yes, I understand." Jasmine's cloudy eyes cleared and she grasped Esther's hand with both her filthy ones, as a drowning person clutches a lifeline.

Esther gave her a long look. "I know you've never liked me very much, Jasmine. But you must trust me now and do exactly as I say if we are to survive."

twelve

High up on the bluffs above the camp, Esther paused along the trail to slip out of the dress she had worn to the tribal celebration feast for the triumphant return of the warriors.

Jasmine curled against a rock, her head drooping onto her chest, still heaving from the exertion of the climb.

"Jasmine, are you all right?" Esther asked, using the brilliant moonlight to examine the deathly pale face. Still, she was relieved to see, the woman's appearance had improved drastically with the advent of hope, plus a thorough cleansing with lye soap in the river.

"No. I'm terrified of what they will do to us when they learn we are gone. I'm sick all over with fright." As if on cue, a shudder rippled through her body, and the hollow eyes regarded Esther through a glaze of fear and fatigue.

"They will not miss us for a long time," Esther said with a bold show of confidence.

Looking down on the brightly moonlit camp from this vantage point, the village appeared as a miniature on a tabletop. She could see the great fire and the tiny figures silhouetted in a circle around it. "See, Jasmine, the whole village is still dancing. The warriors continue riding into the fire circle to tell of their coup. Who counted coup and how many hasn't been decided yet. None will go back to their lodges until that decision is reached."

Esther carefully folded the cream-colored ceremonial dress and soft beaded moccasins and stored them in the pouch tied to their pack horse. Then, slipping into her comfortable, worn buckskins and heavy work moccasins, she tied a knife sheath around her waist. From habit, she tested the sharpness of the blade that had begun as a small kitchen utensil. She had ground it down from the original shape until it was thin as a stiletto and beveled only on one side, well-oiled and razor-sharp. Satisfied with its edge, she slipped the blade into the sheath and fastened her bow and the quiver filled with arrows over her shoulders.

"Jasmine, are you ready to ride?" Esther asked.

There was a puzzled frown on her companion's face. "Do you really think it safe? I do not mind walking, really I do not." Jasmine eyed the large sorrel thoroughbred mare, the blood of centuries of strong, fleet Arabian horses flowing in her veins, and drew away.

Esther managed a tight smile. "I know you do not like horses and you do not like riding, but we can't *walk* all the way."

"All the way . . . to where?"

"Jasmine, I do not know to where." Esther struggled to steady her voice, lest she reveal her own fears and impatience. "Just away from the Comanche. From Tall Lance and his cruelty to you . . . and his determination to kill me."

Jasmine's head bobbed up. "Kill you? Esther, you imagine it. With Running Elk and Makes Medicine sheltering you, no one would dare harm a hair of your head."

"That's the only reason I'm still alive, of course," she admitted. "But Tall Lance just hasn't figured a way to get rid of me yet without the deed being traced to him. But he will, and knowing that Running Elk is planning to make me his wife gives Tall Lance only two more days. I'm convinced that he will try to kill me soon. In fact, he will probably be the first to learn of our escape . . . and then our time will be short."

"You never told me he had threatened you."

"Haven't you noticed the way he watches me? If looks could kill, I would have been dead on the third day of our capture."

"But why would he want to kill *you*?"

"I can only guess." Esther said no more, but privately she blamed Jasmine herself.

Even with two wives, Esther knew Tall Lance was lonely. One wife was hard-working but ugly. The other was a cranky, evil-tempered, lazy crone Tall Lance had married before he knew her disposition. Not only that, but Esther had overheard him confide to Running Elk that he truly longed for a fair woman to love. She suspected that he would have been good to Jasmine if she had not angered him so. To further insult his pride, it now appeared that Running Elk was getting the better end of the bargain—marriage to Esther who was well-versed in Indian ways—while Tall Lance was stuck with Jasmine, who grew uglier and more undesirable by the day.

Yes, Tall Lance wanted to kill her. But when she had tried to discuss his intentions with Running Elk, the war chief had dismissed her fears as those of a silly woman, unworthy of her.

"Esther, can't you please tie me in the saddle like Tall Lance did when he brought me here?" Jasmine asked, clutching the cantle with knuckles whitened from the intensity of her grip.

Her request jerked Esther back to the lonely trail with a start. Quickly fishing out a rope from the pack, she looped it around Jasmine's ankles and pulled her feet tightly against the sides of the horse. Knotting the rope, she slipped the ends under the surcingle holding the spotted cat skin and saddle in place.

"There. Feel more secure?"

"Yes, thank you."

The drums, silent until now, began pulsing through the night air with a steady spellbinding beat, signaling the end of the tales of coup. Now the impartial warriors would weigh the evidence and decide who could and could not count coup. That would take much time. She and Jasmine were safe from discovery for a few hours yet.

Effortlessly, Esther swung into the saddle and gathered the reins. With a departing look over the cliff at the camp, Esther urged the horses up the trail. Very shortly, the path turned into the pass that led out onto the plateau, and the camp disappeared. Only the faint beat of the drums followed them. And as they rode steadily through the night, Esther could not tell when she ceased to hear the beat and when it only pulsed on inside her brain, though she continued to move to its rhythm until sunrise.

The moon was setting as the sun came up. "We must find a place to hide," Esther said. "If we travel at night and rest during the day, our chances of being found are much less."

"Do not you think Running Elk will track you at night?"

"He will, but we must be more clever than he."

Jasmine moaned. "There is *no* one more clever than he. That's why he is the chief."

"Jasmine, where is your faith?" scolded Esther. "God has brought us this far. He won't let us down now if we trust Him. If it is not His will that we stay with the Comanche, He will lead us to safety."

"If it's not His will that we stay with them, then why did He let us be captured in the first place?"

Esther sighed a long sigh. "I've thought a lot about that.

Perhaps we both had some lessons to learn that could only be mastered in this manner."

"What lessons? How to endure hunger and hard work?"

"Yes, and you have come through it all like Job, with your faith in God strong and shining for all to see."

A bitter laugh exploded from Jasmine. "Do not be too sure, Esther. Do not be too sure."

"I *am* sure, Jasmine. You do not know it yet, but I do, else why would you bother to risk everything to escape with me?"

"I keep asking myself that question. I feel the same terror, the same sickness I did when I rode here with Tall Lance. I can't pray. I've given up trying." Jasmine's voice dropped to a whisper and her words ended with a low moan.

"Jasmine, you are the only one condemning yourself. God isn't. And I am not. You have done nothing wrong. Why don't we pray together now?"

Together they bowed their heads, their hands linked in the shadows. "Thank you, Lord, for guiding us and restoring Jasmine. I ask You now for a secure place to spend the day, knowing that You are with us, protecting us from all harm." As Esther finished her prayer, she spotted a dim game trail twisting down the face of bluff to the river. Quickly, she threw her leg over the horse's neck and slipped to ground. "Hang on tight, this path is steep. Here is where we will lose the trackers. Our trail won't be visible for long. The animals going for water will soon wipe away any trace of us."

Esther knew all this for a fact, and her heart sang in thanksgiving.

Late on their fifth night of travel toward the east, Jasmine slept with her head resting against Esther's back, while Esther rode, tense and alert. Besides their extra horse threatening to grow lame, a prickling feeling running along the back of her neck told her that something was different. She did not get the impression of danger; nevertheless, she traveled with considerably more caution than on previous nights.

They were out on the flat prairie now, with no protection except for occasional islands of trees. Tonight large dark clouds scudded across the shrinking moon, blacking out the landscape for periods of time. It was during one of these blackouts that she spotted it—a small wooded area in the distance, with a campfire flickering at the edge.

"Wake up, Jasmine," Esther whispered.

"Uh?" the woman startled.

"There." Esther pointed toward the woods.

Instantly awake, Jasmine's face was a mask of terror. "Oh, Esther, who . . . or *what* do you think it is? We have seen no other humans in five days."

"You stay here with the horses and keep them quiet. I'm going up to see."

"You can't go and leave me alone," Jasmine wailed softly.

"I can't stay with you, either. And we can't take the ponies any closer. Whoever it is will hear their hooves. You're going to have to stay here." Esther looked into wide green pools of fear. "This is the time to pray, Jasmine. The Lord will hear you and give you strength."

"I—I can't."

"Yes, you can," she insisted. "You just haven't tried for a long time by yourself. Get down on your knees . . . but do not forget to hold the reins tight while you do." With those words, Esther, giving thanks for the cover of velvet blackness, crept off toward the fire.

Staying low to the ground and moving with catlike

stealth, she crept across the prairie, covering the distance quickly. Finding a large clump of buffalo grass, she crouched behind it and looked into the camp. Seated cross-legged facing the fire were two men. One, sitting with his back turned to her, wore the uniform of an Army officer, with many stripes on his sleeve. Since his large frame hid the face of the other, Esther crawled on her stomach until she could get a better look.

Savage! She bit back the urge to cry out to him. Though she had thought of him almost constantly, to find him sitting by the fire, relaxed and pensive, seemed like a dream. He was more handsome than she remembered. His face no longer reflected the bitterness she had seen that day in the wood so many months ago. Now, the classic profile, outlined in the fire, held a peaceful look. The flames showed a burnished copper tan from months in the sun. He looked incredibly Indian sitting there, quiet and calm. He was a man totally at ease with himself and the world around. She had been right to love him, right to hold to the hope that he was hunting for her and would find her. Only it was *she* who had found *him*.

The problem now was how to let him know she was here. She did not dare rise and run to him. His reflexes were lightning-quick, and he might shoot her before he realized who she was.

Finally, she found a small rock and pitched it so it landed on the ground next to him. She had been right. In an instant, he had his rifle up and pointed in her direction. Hugging the ground, she called, "It's me, Savage, Esther."

She watched the big man flow to his feet and race in her direction. She only had time to get to her hands and knees before he dropped to the ground in front of her.

"Esther," he whispered and pulled her into the circle of his arms. "Oh, Esther." She felt his sobs, rather than heard them, as he smothered her against his chest in a great crush. "We've hunted for so long and found no trace," he choked and put her away from him.

"My heart sings to see you," she said softly as she wiped the tears from his cheeks. "The prairie is vast, and they left no clues. I watched them circle and retrace their route until everything had been blotted out. No tracker, no matter how good, could have followed us for long." She looked up, staring at him, swept into the depths of his warm gray eyes. "But I knew you were looking," she assured him. "And I knew you'd never give up."

His body was leaner, the angles of his face sharper, more angular than in May, the planes finely etched, revealing firm, strong bones. "You're right about that. Haskell over there was ready to ride back to Fort Leavenworth tomorrow, but he was going alone." His eyes roamed over her, drinking in everything about her. Tension vibrated between them like a plucked bowstring. Her heart rose into her throat and she could barely breathe.

"You're beautiful, Esther Wheeler, more beautiful even than I remembered," Savage whispered in her ear. He put his hand lightly on her hair and captured a stray lock that had escaped its confining braid.

A soft whinny and in a flash, the spell broken, Savage's head whipped around and he reached for his pistol. "Were you followed?"

"I'm sure we have been, but that was my horse you heard. Jasmine is tending her."

"Jasmine is with you?"

"You surely did not think I would leave her behind?"

"I did not think about her at all," he confessed. Turning, he called over his shoulder, "Haskell, there's a lady out there tending a horse. How about going to the rescue?"

Haskell, heaving himself to his feet with a series of grunts, strode off in the direction of the prairie.

"Jasmine, we've found Savage!" Esther called. "Sergeant Haskell is coming out to bring you into camp."

Esther gave thanks that days earlier she had hacked off Jasmine's hair. It now curled over her head in ringlets, clean and unmatted, giving her the look of a thin pixie. Though the travel had been hard, five days with regular food had already improved Jasmine's looks considerably. Tonight she could be seen by the sergeant and Savage without embarrassment.

Savage helped Esther to her feet and guided her toward the fire. "How much time do we have before you figure Running Elk will be here?"

"Not much. I've sensed Running Elk very close several times. We rode in water tonight. There were several streams to choose from, so it will take some time for them to decide which way we went. He isn't alone. He will have the best trackers in the tribe with him."

Savage quickly doused the fire. "That will help some. And there's a storm brewing to darken the moon." He looked up as Haskell and Jasmine arrived in the small clearing. "Esther says the Comanche are hard on their trail. We can't stay here. It will be more confusing if we split up and ride for the fort separately."

Feeling like she was being pulled apart, Esther sank slowly to the ground.

Quickly, Savage knelt beside her. "What's the matter? Are you ill?"

"Yes and no," she said in a trembling voice. "If we ride to the fort, Running Elk will make war to take me back. He and other good men, both white and red, will surely be killed. Let Jasmine and the sergeant go to the fort. Let us track off in another direction. Running Elk knows my pony tracks by now and will follow us. Perhaps we could outrun him."

Savage thought for a few minutes. "I have some ideas," he said at last. "We aren't that far from the Cheyenne. We will be safe once we're in their stronghold."

"Good," she breathed.

Haskell stared at Esther, his undisguised admiration showing in his face. "Name's Haskell, ma'am, Archibald Haskell, late of the U.S. Army."

Esther nodded. "Much obliged for your help in finding us." He was a good man, probably in his late forties or early fifties.

"Seein' you, ma'am, I can sure understand why Savage has tracked you night and day." Turning to face Jasmine just as the clouds uncovered the moon, he bowed, "And you too, ma'am. Nobody told us we'd be findin' *two* beauties."

Jasmine regarded him coldly. "Sergeant Haskell, let's have an understanding right now. I have been starved and worked to near death by a cruel warrior. I am not fit—"

"Mrs. Waite," he interrupted, "I know how Indians treat their white slaves. That you have escaped with any kind of sanity a'tall bespeaks the high type woman you are. I am returnin' to Fort Leavenworth pronto. If you'd like to make the trip with me, I'd be most obliged to have your comp'ny."

One thing Jasmine had learned through her ordeal was to hold her tongue. She stood quietly watching Haskell as he turned a brick red and wiped the sweat from his upper lip.

"Well, Mrs. Waite, what I'm tryin' to say is, I'm an old dog ready to retire. I got no family, no home. I'm lookin' to set up a place and, if after we get to know one another better—" His voice trailed off into an embarrassed silence.

Not a flicker of emotion altered Jasmine's features. She regarded the nervous man for some time before she said, "Sergeant Haskell, I appreciate your offer of an escort to the fort. I will not hold you to anything more. Given time, we shall see about the rest."

Clouds settled over the moon again and flicks of lightning pierced the heavy black clouds. Rumbles of distant thunder beat on the air and a cool wind began blowing. "Looks like a good time for us to move out," Savage said.

"Our pack horse is lame," Esther said. "I do not think he'll stand riding."

"I've a good extra mount," Haskell said, turning to Jasmine. "We can ride double. That is, if you do not mind, ma'am."

She regarded him with heavily lidded eyes. "My name is Jasmine, and I wish you would call me that, Sergeant." Having made the point of her name, she seemed to mellow a bit, and she took a step toward the sergeant. "And no, I do not mind. I'm no horseman, and I find riding alone a terrifying experience."

The sergeant took Jasmine's hand and, as though escorting her to a fancy ball, he led her to his horse. "Since we're goin' to become more than acquaintances, my name is Archibald."

Jasmine smiled the first sweet smile Esther had seen cross her face in months. "A most fitting name for so fine a gentleman."

Esther followed, and the two women embraced with a genuine caring born of months of shared suffering. "Take care of yourself, Jasmine. I have a strong feeling your life is going to take a decided turn for the better."

Jasmine smiled. "Thanks to you and the Lord, I may have

a life to live after all. And, Esther, I must ask your forgiveness for all the things I said about you—" Choked with emotion, she could not go on.

"Have a safe trip, and God go with you." Esther gave her a final hard squeeze and turned away so Jasmine would not see the tears.

Squaring her shoulders and with a dip of her head, Jasmine placed her foot in the stirrup. "Archibald, with a bit of help, I am ready to mount this animal."

Haskell set Jasmine on the skirt of the saddle and climbed on, awkwardly swinging his leg over the horse's neck. Esther handed Savage Jasmine's pitiful little pouch containing her belongings, and he tied it to the saddle. Then, scrounging a blanket from his pack, Savage wrapped it around Jasmine's thin shoulders. She smiled her gratitude and clutched the folds to her.

"Looks like you're ready to ride," Savage observed. "Have a safe trip."

Haskell looked down at the big man, real affection in his eyes. "It's been a great experience, Savage. One I would not have missed for the world. Take care of yourself wherever you and the lady decide to go. Just might run into you one of these days."

Savage held out his hand and the two men clasped wrists. Reluctantly, they drew apart and Haskell placed Jasmine's arms around his waist. "You hang on tight, now. We're gonna make tracks for civilization."

Haskell set his heels against the horse's sides and it took off at a good pace. The thunder covered the sound of the hoofbeats, but lightning, streaking the sky in eerie flashes, occasionally lit the pair as they disappeared into the vastness of the prairie.

Savage put his arm across Esther's shoulders. "Ready?"

"Ready," she said and swung effortlessly onto her horse.

Savage leaped onto his pony, Indian fashion, and turned its head into the wind and the storm. "We'll ride north into Cheyenne country. Pray your Comanche friends have had all the war they want this season and do not follow us."

Esther did not tell Savage that Running Elk would be as determined to have her back as Savage had been to find her. Tracking her into Cheyenne country would only slow him down. It would not stop him.

thirteen

The storm that began so ferociously was a false alarm and passed with nothing more than a spectacular fireworks display. Though it had been a long time since rain and moisture was sorely needed, Esther gave thanks that there had not been a heavy downpour to soak them as they traveled.

They rode in the pale morning light, the weak sun barely penetrating the heavy cloud cover, up the rocky bottom of a wide flat canyon. But it was light enough now for Savage to see her buckskin breeches meeting the tops of her high moccasins, a fringed shirt, and her hair braided in two heavy braids wrapped Comanche style with otter skin. Savage looked . . . no, *studied* the effect.

His eyes kept returning to the red paint down the part in her hair. "You turn completely Comanche?" he finally asked.

Though the words seemed innocent enough, she did not like their implication. Her eyes narrowed as she probed his face. "What are you asking?"

"Painted your part. Means you're married."

"First time I've known you to be wrong, Cheyenne man. You obviously do not know what it means." She searched hard inside to find a balance in her words and voice—enough force to let him know it mattered to her, but not so much intensity that it forced him to defend his words. They knew so little about each other and yet they knew so much. Right now, either one could say something to shatter their fragile love before it matured.

Cautiously, in a more gentle voice, she continued, "All

Comanche women and girls paint their parts for ceremonial events. The red line signifies the long trail I will travel during my lifetime, and asks the Great Spirit to make me fruitful."

She gave him a sidelong look and saw that his profile had relaxed slightly. And since he continued to ride by her side, she was satisfied that he was not angry and had accepted her explanation.

Esther would have liked to talk more with him. There was so much to say, but he seemed drawn within himself, listening, sensing the very air about them. She knew that while he listened politely, until they were safe, she would have only a small part of his attention. Still, she was selfish enough to want it all.

"This valley is the understood border of Cheyenne territory," he was saying. "We should be reasonably safe here. Safer," Savage went on, "than trying to find shelter for the daylight hours inside Comanche country."

As they rode, however, he kept turning to look back over his shoulder.

Growing more nervous by the minute, Esther could not resist asking, "Do you see something to cause alarm?"

"No, but I have an ugly feeling, and I can taste death. It crawls up and closes off my throat."

She felt the color drain from her face and a hollow open in the pit of her stomach. "I guess I'm grateful for your honesty, but what are we to do? Do you think Running Elk knows we are here?"

"I do not think it has anything to do with Running Elk or the Comanches. I do not know what's the matter, but it's very bad. Stay close and do exactly as I tell you . . . when I know what that is." He sent her a rueful smile and his eyes softened as they met hers.

She drew them to her, held them, watched as they traced her face, seeing her heart-shaped browline, high cheekbones, straight nose with finely flared nostrils, lingering on her full mouth and firm chin. His hands flexed and Esther felt his need to touch her. She reached out to him, and he took her hand, holding it as they rode with fingers entwined, letting their love flow and mingle.

They rode a while in the warm glowing silence, then she asked, "Do you still sense something wrong?"

"Yes." This time when he spoke, his eyes and voice suddenly turned hard as flint. "Only it's much worse than I thought."

She pursed her lips and turned around. There was nothing in the canyon but the stream flowing deceptively smooth, gurgling as it bumped up against rocks in its path. "It disturbs me that I feel nothing. I am usually the first to grow uneasy."

"Do you doubt me?"

Her eyes widened. "No. Only myself. If such a great danger exists and I am unaware of it, then I am dangerously vulnerable."

He allowed himself the ghost of a boyish grin, easing the long tension. "Means you'll have to stay close to me at all times."

They stopped to rest at the water's edge and let the horses drink. The water ran dull, reflecting the leaden skies overhead. Crows wheeled like black messengers in and out of the low clouds, cawing crossly at one another. The rest of the land seemed unnaturally quiet. She and Savage made no attempt at conversation. He still seemed to be listening and looking for the unseen danger.

Mounting up again, they rode on up the barren valley. Only random clumps of grass held the sand in place. But it was so tough and old, the horses made no attempt to snatch any as they walked by.

Esther heard the pounding hooves before she saw the lone buffalo stagger into the canyon, fall, struggle to its feet, and crash on again. "Look!" she cried.

Both wheeled their horses around and watched the animal weaving an erratic pattern—stumble and fall, rest while it gathered strength enough to rise, then lurch on until something tripped it up and, helplessly, it crumpled again to the ground.

Savage set his heels in Smoke's ribs and they rode back until they could see the buffalo clearly. The hair had been singed off the animal's back, revealing shriveled skin like dried grapes. Its knees were bloodied, scraped raw by repeated falls as it ran in blind circles over the prairie.

"Look, Savage, his eyes are swollen shut and his face is blistered. Looks like he's been burned."

"The lining of his nose has been seared, and he can't smell. That explains why he's letting us get so close to him."

Esther gave Savage a stricken look. "Poor thing, what can we do for him?"

"He's doomed to attack by wolves or coyotes and, blind as he is, he can't defend himself. Shooting him and putting him out of his misery is the kindest act."

Though she knew Savage was right, Esther did not want to watch. She pressed her hands over her ears and lifted her eyes, looking out the mouth of the canyon to the prairie beyond.

There, reflected by the low somber layer of clouds, was a reddish glow spreading across the horizon. At night around the campfire, Enoch Fisher and others had told of sweeping prairie fires, but their most vivid descriptions had not begun to prepare Esther for the eerie magnificence of this destructively spectacular act of God. Though she jerked at the sound of Savage's rifle, her eyes remained fixed in dazed fascination as the tinted sky grew rapidly brighter.

"Fire!" Her voice was a keening wail.

Savage gave a low moan. "So this is what I've been fearing. Here in the canyon, the wind's been blowing the smoke past us." His broad shoulders slumped and his head bowed. "This could be the end for us," he said and looked at her with tortured eyes.

She nodded her understanding and reached out for his hand.

While they watched, the wind picked up, chasing the flames ever higher before it, sending them roaring into the mouth of the canyon. Too late to escape through the entrance, they were sealed inside, waves of heat beating against their faces. Towering tongues of fire licked at the foreboding clouds turned an orange-red, and filled the canyon with gigantic shadows flickering in grotesque shapes over the red-stained cliffs.

Savage looked at her for a minute, roused from his state of hopelessness, took out his field glasses and searched the walls of the cliffs holding them prisoner. Game, fleeing before the advancing fire, began trickling past. Then the trickle became a flood. The animals that were fleeter of foot—deer and pronghorn sheep—arrived first, racing up along the river, scrambling in terror over the rocks of the cliffs to the high plateau at the head of the canyon.

"Can we follow the animals?" she asked and coughed as the black smoke rolled over them, stinging her eyes and nose. The roar and crackle of the flames echoed against the rocks and still they did not move. "Can't you find some place for us?" she pleaded between coughs.

"Maybe—" He slipped the glasses into their case and pointed to a ledge. "There's a narrow game trail up there and I think I can see a cave. Come on. Let's try to make it."

Seeing her hesitate, Savage reached out and pulled her onto his horse, holding her in the saddle in front of him. Setting his heels in the ribs of the big sorrel, he raced toward the cliffs, towing Esther's horse by its reins.

At the beginning of the rock-strewn trail, Savage reined to a stop, and dismounted. "We'll have to hike up. Trail's too narrow to ride. If a horse spooks, it'll go over the side before one of us can stop it."

Dumbly, she nodded. The narrow trail, steep and rocky, wound between crevices and around huge boulders, dislodged centuries ago from the bluff walls. It took all Esther's concentration to keep her balance and lead the horse. Savage set a grueling pace and she struggled to keep up. She set her jaw, however, and vowed she would not give him the satisfaction of having to stop for breath before he did. The higher they climbed, the more agonizing grew her need until finally only the dull thuds of the horses' hooves echoed over her deep gasps for air.

Esther thought her lungs would burst, but Savage marched on with dogged determination. What on earth made it so necessary that they reach the ledge without stopping? If she had any breath to spare, she would have asked him, but that would have necessitated stopping, and something in the set of his jaw told her he would not do that. Her only consolation was that his breathing was as labored and ragged as her own.

Fire burned through her legs and flowed into her lungs and parched throat. Like it or not, Esther was going to have to stop or fall on her face in the trail.

"Don't . . . think . . . 'bout . . . stopping," Savage read her thoughts. "We're . . . almost . . . there."

"Why can't . . . we rest?" she pleaded.

"I can't be sure . . . and do not want to take the time to look, . . . but I thought I saw a glint of light . . . from the bluff across the canyon. May not be anything and then again—"

Worn from the pace she had set to escape from Running Elk, she had very little left to give, but his words frightened her enough to plod on a bit farther. She bowed her head and looked only at the trail before her. It took every bit of reserve strength she had to pick up her feet and set them a few inches farther along the path. They began to feel like lead weights at the ends of her legs and, when she stumbled and nearly plunged over the side, she was sure she could not take one more step. She lacked the strength or the voice to call to Savage, but looking up she saw the sharp turn the trail made onto the shelf he had described seeing from the ground.

On the ledge, she started to collapse against the bluff wall. Strong fingers dug into her arm and Savage half-dragged her into the cave. Once inside, she slid slowly to the ground, closed her eyes, and curled into a pain-washed heap. She lay like that for many minutes, weaving in and out of consciousness, recovering her wind.

"You all right?" Savage finally asked in a thick croak.

Esther raised her head to answer and saw him slumped against the jagged rock wall, his face gray and strained, his eyes watching her. In one hand he held his field glasses and in the other, he held out the canteen to her.

"Thank you," she said and drank greedily. Wiping her mouth with the back of her sleeve, she handed the nearly empty container back to him. "I was so thirsty, I imagined I heard trickling water."

"Was not your imagination." He staggered to his feet and crossed the hard uneven floor to where a thin stream of water spilled over the rocks and collected in a small pool at the base. He filled the canteen and slaked his own thirst, then filled the flask again.

Moving past her, he brought the horses inside and led them to the pool. They drank in great noisy gulps. Then, he led them into the back of the cave. Fishing around in a pack, Savage returned with something wrapped in oilcloth. "Our meal won't be the most memorable. All we have is some pemmican and hard biscuits."

"I won't complain," Esther said and accepted her portion gratefully. "I've eaten worse."

While they ate in silence, Savage played his glasses across the plateau across from them and Esther stared into the valley below. For want of fuel, the fire had burned itself into smoldering ruin. "See anything?" she asked at last.

He shook his head. "Could have been the fire glinting off a piece of mica." But he did not sound convincing.

The promised storm arrived, the chill breeze stopping briefly to switch directions and return with renewed force to whistle around the cave entrance. It carried with it the acrid scent of the dead fire. A close-by crack of lightning sent the horses dancing against their tethers, and Esther shivered.

Unfolding his long frame, Savage got up and brought the horses closer to the entrance. "Since we do not have wood for a fire, the horses will help keep us warm." He took their saddles off, stacked them together to provide a back rest, then brought the soft wildcat skin that protected Esther's mount from the saddle and handed it over to her. Turning the fur side in, she wrapped it around herself.

"Thank you, Savage," she said simply. "And thank You,

dear Lord," she prayed aloud, "for providing for all our needs again."

"More than you realize," he said. "The fire and now the rain will remove any trace of our tracks. The best tracker in the world will never know what direction we took."

With a deep sigh, she turned to him and found his eyes, wide and shining, gazing at her. "And so, my beloved, we are safe, at last," she said softly.

Tucking the wrap around her snugly, he moved to cup her upturned face in his hands. She closed her eyes, relishing his nearness, and he kissed the delicate lids, the smooth skin of her forehead, and she smelled the slight scent of salt still clinging to his skin. Then he drew her close against him and tenderly stroked her hair, pulled tight at the temples into the thick braids.

Her head nestled in the hollow of his neck, she could feel the quickened beat of his heart as he whispered, "My beloved."

Such an endearment had never been uttered to her, and she trembled with the delight of it, the promise it bespoke.

"You are my beloved, Esther," he said deliberately as though to impress the fact upon her. "I love you as I love life, Esther Wheeler."

"Oh, Savage," she breathed against his lips, "and I love you."

He kissed her then, and she was lost in the wonder of being with him, of having his strength to stand guard over her, of seeing the gray of his eyes turn from cold granite to warm blue-gray, shining with his love. With him, she knew she would never have to face the world alone again.

For one moment more, she kept the other thought at bay, kept him close to her, kept their love whole around her. But

Running Elk's face would not be put aside. It rose before her in all its dark intensity, blotting out Savage.

She stirred and he held her away from him. "What's the matter?" he asked sharply. Then, without waiting for her reply, his voice softened. "I know you have been through much, but you're safe now. Let me do the worrying for a while."

She turned from his arms, and the fear flooded back, draining her, pulsing through her. "Savage, Running Elk won't give up until he's found me. He's a dangerous man, clever and ruthless when he wants something."

"So am I," Savage said, a harsh edge in his voice.

Esther saw the truth of his words born in the change that instantly came over him. His eyes turned cold and deadly under slitted lids, his face again assumed the hardened planes and angles of a killer, and it frightened her.

Then, like a chameleon and as quickly, he again made himself gentle for her. "I must settle one thing before we move on in the morning. Will you marry me?" His voice was soft, but the intensity told her how much her answer meant to him.

"Oh, my dearest, I can't imagine living without you as my husband." She drew his head down once more and kissed him.

Weary from the long days of strain, they moved to separate corners of the cave and slept.

fourteen

The autumn air, crisp and cold, flowed past them in a gentle morning breeze. A bright blue sky with only a few straggling dark clouds was all that remained of yesterday's storm. Outside the cave, the prairie stretched in the distance, black and lifeless, as far as the eye could see.

"What is your plan?" Esther asked, scanning the horizon in all directions.

Savage leaned with his forearms resting on his saddle horn, using his thumb to push back his hat, and let his eyes drift to the north. "We have two choices, maybe three, as I see it. We can keep on going north, hope to find a late wagon train with someone to marry us. We can go east and get married at the first settlement we come to. Or we can turn south for Santa Fe. Your decision."

"South is Comanche and Apache country. That would be too dangerous, even if we were not trying to avoid Running Elk. East means civilization, and one thing this adventure has taught me is that I'm not cut out for settlement living." She cocked her head at him. "You knew I'd choose the north, did not you?"

He grinned a slow grin. "Hoped you would. North is Cheyenne territory, home to me. And I do not think it will be hard to waylay a train. There's always somebody along to do marrying."

"Then let's move out," she suggested. "I've been alone long enough."

With each passing day and no sign of Running Elk or the Comanche, Savage grew less tense. Finally, he agreed it was probably even safe to travel by daylight and, this morning, Esther was seeing for the first time the rugged mountains he had told her so much about. Distorted in a blue haze and at a distance of several days' journey to the West, they still looked imposing.

"At the foot of yonder tallest peak, in the most beautiful canyon you ever laid your eyes on, I had a snug little cabin," he began softly as they stopped to rest the horses. "Had me a fine woman and two babies. Life was sweet and full of promise until five years ago. Came back from a hunting trip to find the Comanche on the warpath—" She listened as his voice grew as hard as the muscles in his clenched jaw. "Burned the cabin to the ground and killed my family. I rode in as they rode out. I won't rest until I get the Indian that did it."

"Do you know who it was?"

"I do not know his name, but I'll never forget his face. He turned around and we both got a good look at one another before he rode away."

"You mean a single warrior attacked your family?"

Savage nodded.

"Isn't that unusual?"

"I've thought a lot about that. But why he did it doesn't matter. He did it, ugly and brutal, and he's going to pay if it takes the rest of my life."

"Why did you wait until now to tell me about this?" Esther asked, bewildered. Then after thinking about Savage's omission for a while, anger surged in her, and she flared at him. "Brook Savage!"

He turned to her, shock at her anger registering in his

widened eyes.

"Hunting down a nameless Indian isn't how I want to spend my life. I love you, but not enough to watch you waste your life and mine on senseless revenge."

"Now wait a minute," he said in a smooth, calming voice. "I did not say I was going to make that my sole reason for living. Just that when the time comes right, I'll get him, and I thought you ought to know." His face paled in the bright sunlight and he looked weary.

"Hard thoughts are heavy burdens," Esther said with determined force. The weight of her words slammed against him and he moved out in front. She followed, still pondering his words. It was not right for a man to carry enough hate in his heart to kill with and yet, she did not know what to do about it. This was something she was going to have to discuss with the Lord. In fact, they would probably have many discussions about this.

She and Savage rode in silence for some distance, then he turned, his face a mask, and asked, "Have you ever heard from your white family?"

His question caught her by surprise and she gulped. "No," she managed evenly. "When I was ransomed in New York, the officials said they would try to get word to my parents. They found out they both were dead, and nobody along the Blue River in Indiana knew what had happened to Saba and Phelan—but the one I really miss is my Aunt Mercy. She was more like a mother to me than Mama. Chances are she's dead, too. Twenty-four years is a long time."

"Two of a kind, aren't we? No family but each other." He reached out and took her hand. "I promise never to give you any cause to be sorry after we're married."

There it was again. She could not run from it this time. "You've made two promises today, Brook Savage, and you can't keep them both. You have to give up your vow to kill the Comanche, or you will cause me sorrow."

He did not look at her, but dropped her hand and rode on ahead. After a long time, he fell back and rode along beside her once more. "I can promise I won't go looking for him. But . . . if he comes across my path—" Savage paused to see how she was taking it— "I'll have to kill him. Something in me won't let him live after what he did to my family—" He flexed his jaw. "I can't let that . . . atrocity . . . go unpunished."

Perhaps the paths of the two men would never cross. She could always pray for that. "I do not like what you're saying, but I don't want to live without you either." Was she going to be sorry she did not take a stand over this, make him promise to give up his vendetta? She was not even sure she would win. He could possibly live his life without her. But, to her, life without Savage was unthinkable!

A slight smile altered his stern features. "Probably such a bad Indian he's already been done away with by some enraged settler. The coward's bones have most likely been picked clean long ago by a flock of vultures."

"I can hope . . . and pray," she said softly.

They camped this night in a deep ravine and Esther felt safer than she had since the night in the cave. When an arrow hissed through the air and buried itself in the muscle of Savage's upper arm, he made no sound beyond a sharp grunt.

Shocked awake, she stifled a scream and crawled from her side of the flickering fire to where he lay. "Hold still. Let me see," she whispered.

"Leave it," he ordered in a low rumble, pain weakening the usually rich timbre of his voice. "Let him think he killed me.

He'll come closer to have a look. Then I'll shoot the miserable cur."

"You could bleed to death before then."

Another arrow whirred through the silent night, landing just above Esther's head. Slowly, moving only her eyes, she looked around. "We're in deep shadows. I do not think anyone can see. I think they're shooting in the general direction of the horses and getting lucky."

"Any luckier, and we're going to be dead." Savage reached up and pulled the arrow out of the dirt.

Esther gasped and grabbed it from him. The base of the shaft was marked with two narrow red lines. "Running Elk! He's found us. This is his brand on the arrow."

"You're going to have to run for it!" Savage whispered to her. "I'll hold them off."

"No, you do not know how many are out there. I'm staying with you."

"I've had one woman cut to ribbons by Comanche, I'll not have another, no matter what the cost. You've got no chance at all if you stay." A tender look of pleading filled his eyes. "Please go."

"I can't leave you alone, wounded and helpless. Do not ask me to."

"Esther, listen to me. This is our only chance to get out of here alive—" He grimaced with pain. "I have plenty of ammunition and water. They're not going to do anything until morning, so I can last until you bring help. If you ride straight to Bent's Fort, you'll be back long before things even get interesting."

"Well, I'm not going until I fix that arm."

He sighed. "You are a stubborn woman."

When she had broken off the shaft and pulled it through,

she saw that the arrow had only grazed Savage's arm. He was not badly hurt, and she offered continuous prayers of thanksgiving while she packed his wound with herbs she had brought with her in her flight.

"Cover your hair with my hat. That white mane of yours reflects moonlight as well as sunlight." He kissed her hard, letting his longing for her speak volumes. "Now, go!"

Esther clamped Savage's plains hat on her head and crawled to where the horses were tethered and still saddled. A few stray wisps of cloud briefly darkened the moon and, leading her horse by the reins, she set off in darkness through the night. The trail was too steep and treacherous to ride and, on foot, it seemed hours before she broke out on top and could mount up.

Once on horseback, she fled through the hollow of a hill, then struck out across the gently rolling plateau. The moon, though not full, still gave light enough to see by. The cool air of the night, the slow sweep of stars overhead, their slight swaying as she rose and fell in the pulsing rhythm of the gallop, reassured her, little by little.

She was going to get away and bring back help. She was. Glory be to God, she *was*! She gave the pony her head and they rode on like an arrow, straight and true. The hills swept by, an occasional tree whirred past, the pounding hooves of the pony struck sparks from the rocks, here and there.

When, at last, she could feel the sorrel's sides heave in great waves as she sucked in air and her head bobble slightly, Esther knew the pony was used up. She pulled in on the reins. Gradually, the little animal's stride slowed from a full gallop to a stumbling walk. It was then Esther heard the beat of hooves well behind her. Her heart stopped. Had Savage made a break for it and followed her? Inside, she laughed bitterly at her wishful thinking.

Perhaps it had not been Running Elk following them, after all. It could be a bunch of renegades. But if so, she was in worse trouble. How did they get Running Elk's arrows? The only obvious answer was that they had killed him and taken them. Fear pounded in her head and dried her mouth. She must find a place to hide and find it quickly.

A small thicket appeared ahead. Probably growing around a spring, she thought. It would have to do. There was nothing else on the flat rolling landscape to offer any kind of protection.

As Esther rode closer, she heard the trickle of water. Dismounting, on moccasined feet she walked silently until she found a small stream that pooled itself conveniently in the lap of a sunken boulder, well hidden by a tangle of brush. Esther led the horse inside the willows and tethered him. Looking and waiting, she listened intently to see if she really was being followed, or if what she had heard was only the product of an active imagination. Though she heard nothing more, that gave her no comfort.

They both drank, Esther and the pony, letting the cool liquid ease down and relieve raw parched throats. Making no sound, she stood against the animal and listened again. If there had been hoofbeats, they had stopped. There was no sound except the occasional howl of a wolf, lonely and far away.

At last, she slowly sank to the ground and rested her head on a stump-sized rock. The fright gradually drained away and, exhausted, she nodded, almost asleep, until something startled her wide awake. She listened, holding her breath, but the only sounds close by were the pony's breathing. Yet, she felt warned of danger, as though an invisible guard posted near her had heard what her sleep-dulled senses had failed to register.

Fear gripped her again, rendering her immobile, a motionless statue. She raised her head a bit at a time. And then she saw an indefinable form glide through the shadows straight toward her. On all fours, it was impossible for her to distinguish what or who it was. Too late to run, she clenched her fists and waited, a cold smear of perspiration beading on her forehead and in the palms of her icy hands.

She did not stir, did not move a muscle. Even the pony seemed to know something was amiss, for he stopped eating the tender ends of the willows and stood, unmoving.

Without warning, a hand dropped like a mask over her face, a hard, damp hand like cold stone. Her jaws locked. She could neither move nor cry out. For the tenth part of a second she prayed it was Savage, then the familiar scents of smoke, rancid grease, and sweat told her it was not. His other hand, with fingers like steel thongs, pulled her up hard against his tall lean figure and held her so tightly she could barely drag in enough air to keep from fainting. As she weakened, she felt the grip loosen and he spun her around and dropped his smothering grip.

Running Elk! How had he known where to find her? Had he killed Savage? She refused to consider that possibility. Other questions darted through her head like bats in the twilight, but she did not dare ask.

"I am sorry I frightened you," he said surprisingly tenderly. "I did not know it was you for sure. With your hair covered and dressed in buckskins, you looked like a man. I have come to take you home." He spoke without rancor.

Esther did not know how to answer. But she must deal with him honestly. Best to get it over with, cut quick and clean iike a sharp knife. "Running Elk, the White Eyes did not capture me. I willingly went with him. I love him."

The only indication that Running Elk had even heard her was a slight narrowing of his eyes. "You are mine. I gave many horses to Makes Medicine for you. He is white, you are Indian. He cannot make you happy."

"Please, Running Elk, you have been very good to me and I care greatly for you, like a sister for a brother. But it is Savage I love."

"You cannot be sure of that. Away from here, you will forget him and be happy with the People." He untied the reins of her horse and took her by the wrist. "Come, you walk first. I will come behind and lead your horse." He continued to talk to her smoothly, gently, as one would quiet a startled animal.

She obeyed, not wanting to inflame his wrath, but her brain struggled desperately. She must think of a way to escape and get on to Bent's Fort. Other people had been in situations as desperate as this and devised ways out. She had to think, keep calm and think. *Please Lord, let me know a plan that I may save Savage and escape from Running Elk. And let there be no bloodshed.*

From behind, Running Elk directed her over the prairie, first to the left, then to the right, until they came to another clump of trees. Tethered inside were three magnificent horses. She immediately recognized the one wearing a saddle as Raven. The other two carried small packs. She brushed an aimless hand against Raven's shoulder, rippling and hard with muscles.

"What do you plan to do?" she asked, facing Running Elk.

"Does this man you call Savage love you, also?" Running Elk asked with a serious face.

"Yes, he does."

"And you find only the love of a brother for me?"

"You know I find you very dear. But I cannot make my heart feel what it will not."

Slowly, he nodded. "If that is all you have in your heart to give, I will not ask more. Someday, perhaps, you will come to love me as a woman loves a man. I can wait. These last days have shown me I cannot live without you. Even the crumbs of your affection will serve to keep me warm."

Esther started to speak, but the hard look in his eyes silenced her.

"We will lay a trail that Savage will have to follow."

Her heart leaped with gladness that her beloved was alive, then Esther frowned as the meaning of Running Elk's words came clear. "You are using me to bait a trap for him?"

"You will never love me while he is alive."

"And I will never love you if you kill him."

"It will be a fair fight. The victor will have you for himself."

"Running Elk, that is barbaric!" she exploded. "I will not be the spoils won in battle."

He looked with great tolerance at her. "You have no choice."

"Savage will not come after me," she said, gambling that perhaps he would stay put until she and Running Elk were too far away to track.

The corner of his mouth lifted, and fine lines of amusement deepened around his eyes, telling her how ridiculous he thought her words. "If this is a real man who loves you, nothing will keep him from tracking you for as long as it takes to get you back. He is going to come in a rage, blaming himself for letting you go for help. Oh, yes, my beautiful Esther, he will come. And his rage will be grand to behold!"

fifteen

Late in the afternoon, Esther and Running Elk came off the shoulder of the plateau and saw before them the western pass between granite peaks. The walls stood close together on either side, making a thin slit in the mountain. As they entered the pass, Esther had the feeling they crossed a threshold over which neither of them might ever return.

They rode slowly, Running Elk making no attempt to cover their tracks until they came to the creek. From the upper rim of the nearly sheer walls of the canyon it had cut, they looked up and out across naked rock. With difficulty now, for the stream descended rapidly through a series of box canyons, they followed it down from the pass.

Esther would never have guessed it possible, but they worked their way down one after another of the precipitous walls that bordered the creek until, in the canyon below, they came to fine level meadows and groves of lofty pines. Some of these great ancient trees, their fragrance released by the day's heat, lifted their dark green heads above the top of the valley walls.

Esther drew in a sharp breath of delighted surprise at the scene spread before her. A cool green valley rested, gemlike, in a setting of ragged mountains and blue strand of river that flowed through its length. Though she was touched by the view, it was the sound that held her conscious attention. It hung continually in her ears, at first only a thin murmur in the distance, growing deeper, fuller like the deep rumble of drums or the trampling of thousands of buffalo in stampede as they drew near.

Running Elk turned to her. "At the other end of the valley, the river drops in a small rapids, pauses a moment on a wide rock ledge, then falls a great distance."

Esther nodded her acknowledgment. "It grows dark. Is it safe to travel this canyon in so little light?"

"Only a little farther, then you will see."

They rounded a protruding rock and came into a spacious canyon spread with a carpet of thick grass, interrupted by small groves of tall trees. In a gap in the trees stood a log cabin, the sawed ends of unpeeled logs still showing traces of unweathered yellow. Esther's heart leaped. People! Perhaps she could tell someone her plight and they could help her. Slowly, she shook her head. For the sake of the occupants, she should pray that the cabin was empty. In Running Elk's present mood, he would be more likely to kill them for sport.

They hid the horses well back among the trees. "Will you go with me as an Indian, or run screaming a warning as a White Eyes?" he tested.

Here it was again. Would she always have to face this question? How comforting it must be to have clear, undivided loyalties, never to question which side was right, never to know the torment of being torn between two worlds. Would she ever have even a measure of peace? She would not warn the people, she told him, and prayed no one was home.

Running Elk led the way, his noiseless steps pressing down the pine needles without so much as a whisper. Cautiously Esther followed him, taking care that her feet fell in the same spots, across the open ground and into the grove of smaller trees that surrounded the house.

Without challenge, the two of them emerged into the

clearing where the cabin stood and found that the cleared area continued, unobstructed, to the edge of the river. Here, the water seemed to slow and widen, creating a calm surface that reflected the gold of evening. Close to the shore, however, the current constricted in a narrow channel and poured with undisguised speed toward the unseen cataract.

Part of the shoreline was clear of brush, forming a small beach where a small canoe rested, turned bottom-side up. A pile of rugged rocks thrust up close to where the trees began again. A perfect place to keep watch, Esther thought.

Fading off into the trees on their left, they continued on toward the cabin. Running Elk held his rifle, Joseph's rifle, and motioned for Esther to look in the windows of the one-room cabin. Crouching along the wall, she crept up and peered in. She could see only shadowy forms of furniture. The room was empty, she signed to him.

Slowly, they inched their way around to the front door that faced toward the water. Stationing himself on one side of the door and her on the other, he nodded for her to lift the latch. With fingers numb and rigid with fear, she grasped the latch and raised it. The door creaked open, the sound drowning out even the roaring of the falls in Esther's ears. Frozen, she hugged the wall until Running Elk dashed inside waving his rifle.

She could hear him poking around, then he stuck his head outside. "It is empty. Come in."

Still unsure, she stepped into the doorway and surveyed the small room. Even in the afterglow, she could see the furnishings, sparse but neat. She ran her finger over the table to test for dust. There was only a thin covering. She eyed the cold fireplace.

"Do you want a fire?" she asked and picked up the poker.

Indecision flickered in Running Elk's face.

"If we are being followed, and I doubt it," she reasoned, "you have the advantage of being inside the cabin. Unless the owner returns and becomes unhappy at our presence in his home, I do not know why we should not be comfortable."

"You have a silver tongue, Golden One. Build your fire."

It took little to shave some wood curls and place on some wood from a neat stack at the side of the rock fireplace. Soon the fire crackled and cast flickering light through the room.

A narrow bed stood against the far wall, covered with a neatly spread khaki blanket. The earthen floor pounded hard was swept, but bare except for a small, round rag rug next to the bed. A plain undecorated washstand held a thick crockery bowl and pitcher, empty of water now. In the center stood a small square table with two chairs drawn up across from each other. An unlit lamp filled with oil waited in the center of the table to be lit. The most uncommon thing, however, was a small shelf of books on the wall above the bed. Whoever lived here was a person of exceptional taste.

"I will bring the horses up and stake them behind the cabin. When Savage comes, he will not see them," Running Elk said.

"You are so sure he will come. I do not think he will."

Running Elk gave her a disdainful look. "If you speak true and he loves you, he will come. Nothing will keep him from you, just as nothing has prevented my tracking you to the ends of the earth to reclaim you. He and I think much alike."

Without reply, she gathered the water pail from inside the door and followed Running Elk out, each attending to their separate errands.

The fire blazed warm and cheerful, and Esther raked some coals to the outside and set a spider to heat. From the supplies in the packs, she set out the makings of fry bread, but before she began, something drew her to the doorway. Looking out, she watched Running Elk mount the pile of rocks. Then he sat absolutely still, the rifle resting across his knees. The last golden rays of daylight played over his magnificent body and turned him to bronze. The only movement was his lone eagle feather riffling slightly in the evening breeze. From the top of the rock heap he could survey the upper reaches of the river, the clearing, and the cabin itself.

In spite of herself, Esther looked on him with an odd feeling of admiration and awe comingled—admiration for his steadfast devotion to those for whom he felt affection, and awe for the lengths to which he would go to preserve his extended family. He frightened her much of the time, for he hardly seemed human, moving soundlessly, appearing like an apparition out of nowhere, looking so fierce in his war paint.

She sensed the man before she saw his shadow glide, unveering as a compass point to north, across the clearing toward the rocks and Running Elk. *Savage!* She slammed her fist against her mouth to stifle a cry as Running Elk leaped up with a shout and dropped back out of sight among the rocks of the stone heap.

Savage, as though at a signal, sprinted straight forward. Esther clasped her throat and hugged herself to still the trembling. Stripped to the waist, he attacked Running Elk, though she could see no sign of a weapon as he raced toward the warrior.

Running Elk's rifle rang out. Esther shuddered and half-closed her eyes. When she recovered enough to look again, she saw that Savage had not fallen. Instead, he sprinted on until he crouched in the shelter of the steep-sided rocks to catch his breath.

Then, barehanded, Savage swarmed over the barrier with the sure-footedness of a panther on toward where Running Elk waited, armed. The rifle spoke again. Esther shut her eyes and with her knuckles pressed her lips against her teeth to drive back the screams. At such close range, it was impossible for Running Elk to miss.

Hearing nothing, she squinted again at the scene. Savage was still working his way toward the crest of the rocks. Running Elk must not have had a chance to properly load and aim the rifle. She knew he longed for his reliable bow and arrows strapped securely to Raven's saddle. With them, there would have been no missing, and Savage would be dead.

The man was mad to expose himself like that. A few more inches, and he would be in full view of Running Elk. One well-placed bullet . . . Esther dared not think, dared not imagine the burning passion that had mastered Savage, whipped him into such a state.

His towering rage was not spawned by any treatment she had received at Running Elk's hands, for Savage knew that the chief had never been anything but kind to her. Some unspoken fire must burn deep inside him, a driving flame that Savage believed only Running Elk's violent death would quench.

A dark outline rose up on top of the rocks, silhouetted a moment against the turquoise of the darkening sky, then Running Elk's powerful figure joined Savage. The two grappled fiercely, twisting and turning, roaring and snarling above the sound of the falls like two maddened lions. She could not even guess which throat uttered which sound, they were so much alike.

Forward and backward, the closely entangled bodies swayed, and then she saw them lean out, stagger, and fall down the sheer face of the rock into the current of the river!

Unable to stand the uncertainty, Esther threw caution to the wind and dashed across to the clearing. Rounding the side of the rock, she expected to see them both knocked senseless. To her amazement, she found them still struggling. Even in the icy water, as the swift current swept them downstream, they fought, twisting over and under the water, rising to surface and hammer at each other again.

It was as if two mountain lions had gripped one another, and rather than relinquish the win to the other, would allow themselves to be swept to their deaths.

And death lay straight ahead for them both.

Perhaps a hundred feet below the rock, the river disappeared into a raging cataract. Here the water dashed around and over sharp rocks, dove into pools, and swirled out again to pound itself into white foam against more rocks lower down. It was sufficient to grind life from even the strongest.

Paying the danger no heed, the pair, ignoring the current and their impending doom, struggled on. Esther raced ahead and stood at the verge of the plummeting water, looking in horror at the arching water, felt the spray fly against her face, heard the hungry roar pour upward and fill her ears with a death chant.

"Savage!" she screamed. "Running Elk!" Her words, battered and distorted by the river's fury, fell impotent at her feet.

Just above the brink of the falls was a foam-rimmed shoal in the middle of the current. Somehow the two struggling figures were thrown up on it. They rose up out of the water, boiling about their knees, and weaved uncertainly as they stood on the slick rocks. If they took even one step and staggered in the slightest, they would be swept over the precipice. The river pulled and churned around them, struggling to carry them down.

But they fought on, heedless of the danger. Death was in their hearts, one for the other, and it left no room for fear or mercy.

Esther stood watching the fighters twist and turn, grappling, swaying, first one giving, then the other. Reason fled as she watched and her heart spoke. She must try to stop them, and she waded in. When the cold water reached her waist, she sucked in her breath.

Savage was the first to spot her. A look of terror rearranged his features as he froze. Seeing his opponent stricken, Running Elk's gaze followed and registered a similar emotion as he watched Esther struggle toward them.

The men let go each other and reached to drag her up on the shoal.

The first to regain his voice, Savage screamed at her. "What in the name of all that's holy are you doing? You want to get yourself killed?"

"What is life without you in it?" she gasped out. "One of you will not leave this place alive. Maybe both of you!"

"You do not understand!" Savage shouted, turning to face Running Elk. "This is the man who killed my wife and babies! He did not wait until I was around to make it a fair fight. He came while I was away hunting and butchered 'em. Their bodies are buried right over there—" Savage clenched his fists and pointed to the copse of trees behind the cabin.

So Savage had lived here. This was his home.

Then he spat his contempt of Running Elk. "I swore I'd kill the man who did those things. It's taken me five years to find you, Running Elk, to be sure it was you who slaughtered helpless women and children—"

Esther felt the color drain from her face and her stomach rolled over. A slow sick horror rose inside and filled her. In her short time with the Comanche, she had seen such attacks as Savage had described, but she also had seen what white men could do to Indian villages.

"I can understand Savage's hatred, though I do not approve," she told Running Elk in her limited Comanche. "But why do you fight *him* with such venom?" she demanded. "I know there is something more than your attraction to me."

Running Elk's face twisted into a grimace of defiance. He spoke in clipped sentences, making his meaning clear with signs and gestures. "We were hungry. The buffalo did not come and we had to hunt far from our usual places, too close to White Eye settlements. We left the main camp and made a small camp closer to the buffalo, but the White Eyes watched our camp. When they were sure all the warriors were gone, they attacked. There were only seven warriors in the camp. The rest were old men, boys, women, and children. The White Eyes were not content to kill those in the camp, they ruined all the meat, too. Many more of the People died of hunger that winter, slain as truly as if White Eyes had taken knives to their throats."

Esther felt the blood rush from her head, and she swayed. "Were you there?" she asked Savage in a thick voice.

"I was not there," he snorted. "Though the Cheyenne are enemies of the Comanche, I would not commit such a coward's act."

Running Elk did not waver in the intensity of his speech. "When I returned from the hunt, I found all my family dead. My mother . . . my bride of a few weeks—" He paused, shaken by the gruesome memory. "In grief, we rode out, scouring the countryside for any White Eyes we could find. We killed and killed. I do not know where or who." He turned for the first time and lifted glazed eyes to Savage. "I do not remember ever being here before."

Savage stared back. "I do not believe you. You came to this spot today straight as an arrow. You did kill my family, and you remember it. And just as surely, I will kill you."

Esther grabbed Savage's arm and looked full into his face. "Have you ever deliberately killed a man?"

"In war, a few, and I've shot some Comanche and Sioux."

"But not this way. Not toe to toe, with your bare hands, strangling the life from a man."

"No. I've been lucky."

Her eyes widened in surprise. "*Lucky*! You say you are lucky because you have not killed a man in cold blood. How strange to put it that way."

"And why do you think it isn't luck?"

The cold from the water began seeping into her bones. Through chattering teeth, she said, "It could be compassion. It could be righteousness."

A violent laugh exploded from Savage.

"I noticed the Bible on your bookshelf. I think your luck is conscience. Thou shalt not kill!" She dropped her hold on his arm. "Savage, if you do this thing, it will be murder. You will live with murder in your heart, a useless murder that will not bring back your wife or your children."

She turned to Running Elk, speaking haltingly in his tongue. "And killing Savage will not bring back your bride. This barbaric act will accomplish nothing for either of you."

Savage leaned toward her slightly. Without touching her, he searched her face. Esther filled her eyes with all the pleading in her soul, her lips trembling with her desire to speak the words that would free him from his vow.

"You do not understand. You can't know what was done to her, to my children. The mutilation—"

Then Running Elk exploded. "Shall we compare torture for torture, that of the heathen Indian against the civilized White Eyes? Strange that *you* are the man called Savage."

Savage looked at Running Elk. "I will not change my mind. I searched until I found the man who took his vengeance on my family. You could have done likewise. But, instead, you spilled the blood of innocent people. For that, Running Elk, I will kill you."

Each word Savage spoke dropped like chips of ice into Esther's heart. "That is your last word?" she asked.

He nodded.

"Then, hear me well. If you do this thing, I cannot marry you. This thing that has no righteousness in it would always stand between us. There is not enough love in any marriage to live with murder. If you love me—" Her voice filled with anguish so deep she could not continue for a moment. She drew herself tall and held rigid against the pounding of the current against her thighs. "Love," she said and her voice broke, "love ought to guide you."

Savage did not move. His shoulders grew slack as with a heavy burden, and a tired look swept his face. When he spoke, his lips moved stiffly. Esther could not tell if it was from cold or emotion.

"I wish it could be different." He gazed at Running Elk's limp figure, for the moment drained of fury. "He understands and would do the same in my place."

Running Elk nodded. "We will not fight more in your presence, but Savage is right. It must be done."

She looked helplessly from one to the other. "You are crazy, both of you. You do not want to kill each other ... and yet you will." The pain of it at last crumpled her, and she fell sobbing onto the wet rock.

Savage fought upstream against the current and onto the bank. Finding a rope from his pack, he cast it to Running Elk who tied it around Esther's waist. With Running Elk to guide her and Savage to man the rope, they made it safely to shore.

With scarcely any effort, Running Elk picked her up and carried her to the cabin. Savage produced a towel while Running Elk built up the fire. Numbly, she watched Savage turn back the covers on the cot, and both men left the room. Struggling, she stepped out of the soggy buckskins. She toweled dry and slipped between clean blankets.

Exhaustion quickly overtook her, but her last conscious thoughts were of two men working together to save her life. How was it that they could still plan to fight to the death tomorrow? One thing Esther knew for a certainty. She would not be here to witness it.

sixteen

When Esther awoke the next morning, she realized that it had not been early enough. In the first light, she could see fresh clothes laid over a chair—a pair of Savage's buckskin leggings, a shirt she recognized as Running Elk's, and a pair of knee-high fringed moccasins she had left in the village. She tried to imagine Running Elk slipping past Savage, into the cabin, and carefully, lovingly placing her things on the chair.

Maybe they had already had their fight and Running Elk had won!

Throwing back the blankets, she leaped to her feet. The air was unnaturally warm, and she looked at the fireplace. A small fire burned quietly on the hearth, enough to take the chill from the room, and on hot coals at the side of the fire box, a pot of water steamed. When she approached it, there on the table sat a tin plate, the kind Savage carried. On it were two biscuits and a rounded heap of blackberries for her breakfast.

Her heart raced, pulsing blood into her temples so that she could scarcely hear or see. Savage was not dead! Had they, during the night, worked out their differences, called a truce? Were they now friends? Though that was highly unlikely, Esther still prayed so as she quickly washed and dressed.

She looked a moment at the food, considering it, but her throat constricted and she knew nothing would go down. Opening the silent, now-oiled door, she stepped into the morning and looked upriver across the clearing.

Like duelists, they faced each other.

A chill dawn mist rose off the river, coiled around and through the dark branches of the guardian pines. The dawn sky turned pearly as the sun washed the darkness away, and the dark river hissed along its channel as it hurried into foaming ruin over the cataract.

The two men, stripped to breechclouts and armed with knives, stood slightly crouched, taking the measure of each other.

Esther's Indian upbringing took over. Though thoroughly confused by the scene she had awakened to, she well understood what was happening at this moment. Having made a truce earlier to care for her, they were now going to continue their duel to the death, the duel she had only succeeded in delaying last night.

They had certainly chosen the best time of day for it. The sun, not up yet, would not shine in a man's eyes and the air, still crisp from the cool of the night, kept a man's senses sharp and alert.

Slowly, they circled. Savage stood, balanced on the balls of his feet, his right hand holding his knife waist-high, his left hand stretched out to the side, the fingers spread slightly, the hand weaving in small circles. He shifted lightly in response to Running Elk's movements, circled one slow step at a time, moving sideways, keeping just out of reach, then back to the other side, stepping as gracefully as a ballet dancer.

Hugging the wall of the cabin, Esther wanted to run, to leave forever this place of death, but she could not move. Deliberately, she was being drawn into their battle until it seemed she became a part of their circle, found her body moving slightly with the rhythm of their maneuvering. A rhythm as strong and irresistible as if it were being guided by drums.

Strange, but she did not feel hatred flowing between the two men. Not like last night when the air hung thick enough to taste, permeated with their hostility. Esther scrutinized the scene through narrowed eyes, but with surprising calm, her head to one side, as she tried to understand. Involuntarily she licked her lips to taste the air. It held only the scents of autumn—leaves colored and falling, the last berries ripening, the touch of smoke from the fire inside. Downwind from the men, there should have been something radiating from them—hate, fear, anger.

When the reality hit her, she rocked slightly. They did not want to fight each other! Somewhere between last night and now, they had lost their hatred, their desire for vengeance. Savage and Running Elk were only going through the motions, trapped, not knowing how to renounce their vows and still save face.

Esther passed her hand over her brow and shut her eyes. Stopping them was up to her, and she had not the faintest idea how to go about it. *Help me to know, dear Lord,* she pleaded.

At a slight shuffling sound, her eyes flew open. A blade streaked out like the tongue of a snake, and the tip pricked Savage's arm, drawing blood. Esther clapped both hands over her mouth to smother the scream rising inside.

Slowly, the two warriors continued to circle, then a brief glitter, and a small stream of blood trickled over Running Elk's chest.

Think, Esther, think! You must think of something and be quick about it. Lord, where are You? What am I to do?

All the beginning feints were made, and both men had drawn blood. Having taken the measure of each other, what came now would be final.

Running Elk shuffled around an imaginary pivot point.

Savage followed him. The Comanche warrior feinted, then leaned in quickly, his knife ripping upward in a strong, swift motion. Savage knocked the glittering blade away, and Esther watched Running Elk draw in his breath, saw the knife flash briefly as he bent to recover it. Then, he stepped forward and thrust, narrowly missing Savage's thigh.

She could watch no more. Her mind, numb with despair, refused to conjure up a way out for Savage and Running Elk, and she could hear no directions in her heart from the Lord. The two people she loved most on this earth were intent on killing each other, and she was helpless to stop them.

For the first time, she understood the Indian custom of chopping off a finger to ease the pain of grief. Any kind of physical pain right now would have been welcome. It could not begin to hurt with the intensity of the clawing, tearing, shredding her spirit and heart were experiencing.

Their total concentration on each other made Running Elk and Savage oblivious to anything beyond their circle. With the mist still shrouding the clearing, she easily made her silent way to where the horses were tethered. It was not until Esther brushed her face as she reached into a pack for food and felt her damp cheeks that she realized she was crying.

She had not felt this lost and lonely since she was six and had awakened in the bottom of a canoe, an Indian captive, realizing she would never see her family again.

Making no effort to stem the flow, tears dripped off her jaw and wide splotches spread across the delicate dress. Esther did not care. She really wanted to die. Then she looked at trembling fingers fumbling to tie food and water to her saddle and knew that was not true. She wanted desperately to live, and she wanted both Savage and Running Elk alive, too, unharmed and forgiving.

As she led her horse along a faint path away from the river, she came to three graves marked with freshly painted white crosses. He had done that this morning.

Kneeling, she read the inscriptions. This was the resting place of Savage's wife and two sons. Would there be another grave in the small plot by tonight? A family united in death?

No longer able to hold back the sobs, Esther rested her head on the larger cross and cried, deep, wrenching sobs that shook her body and tore at her throat.

Men! They were the most impossible creatures on this earth. Whatever had God been thinking of when He created the unreasonable things? There was no understanding them and no way to stop loving them.

Wiping at the decreasing flood, Esther mounted the patient little pony and continued on along the shadow of a trail nearly invisible in the mist. This must be the way Savage had come last night. When she and Running Elk had arrived at the cabin, she knew there surely had to be an easier trail than the one he led them down yesterday.

Breaking free of the trees, Esther could see a switch-back trail along the face of the mountain. The horse, sure-footed and sturdy, climbed up out of the autumn-touched valley. Though she could see for miles, she forbade herself to look down into the clearing. She had enough terrible memories. She did not need to see one of the dueling pair lying on the ground, his bright shining life draining away in a river of red pooling at the feet of the victor.

She meant it when she had said she loved Running Elk like a brother. But Savage—he was different. She loved him as a man, deeply. She had trusted him completely. How could he throw away their life together in order to satisfy a futile grudge, one he no longer even cared about? Her head hurt from trying to understand.

Stopping her horse on the rim of the canyon, she put all her frustration, grief, rage, and love into a chilling Delaware war whoop. It rang through the canyon, echoed over the roar of the falls, drifted over the clearing. Again Esther let the cry rip from her throat, sat ramrod-straight, staring across the canyon to the west. Then, still without looking down to the valley and clearing below, she turned east toward the prairie.

Unable to bear more grief now, she shut down her mind and sat huddled in the saddle, mute and staring, just riding.

Esther rode like this through the day, some of the time letting the horse have its head, at other times coming to life and in a frenzy of grief, galloping over the canyon-cut plateau like a person crazed.

In the late afternoon the sky clouded over and, with the coming of night and no moon, it grew too dark to safely travel longer in unfamiliar territory. Hearing water, she searched until she saw a glint through the trees and rode up to a pool of clear water.

With a weary sigh, she slid from the saddle and let the tired horse drink. Then she knelt on the stiff dry grass beside the pool. After drinking and splashing the cool water over her burning face, she felt better. Not enough, however, to be hungry. She tethered the horse on a long rope and spread a blanket on the ground under some scrubby evergreens. She took another to spread over herself. Crawling between the scratchy wool, she longed for the soothing fur of the wildcat skin under her saddle. But, if necessary, she wanted the horse ready to ride immediately. With a deep sad sigh, she curled into a ball, more miserable than she had ever been in her life.

God, I've been praying all day and You haven't heard a word I've said. Please, help me. Help them. Let me know You

are listening. I can't stand being cut off from You this way.
Esther continued to plead for guidance and could not
remember when the words stopped going around inside
her head.

Shocked awake by the thunderous blast of cold wind-
whipped rain slamming into her, she sat bolt upright and
denied at first that she had slept. Shaking her head to clear it,
she wrapped the blanket more tightly around herself and
huddled against the storm.

Icy rain puddled around her until she was thoroughly
soaked. *Might as well ride,* she decided. *It won't be as
miserable as sitting here without shelter.*

The blanket on the ground was too heavy with water for
her to lift and she left it. She struggled into the saddle,
keeping the other blanket for protection, though it dripped its
burden of rain. Grateful she had left the horse saddled, she
rode into the black of the storm.

Having no destination, she gave the horse his lead. The
Arabian was strong and plodded on gallantly even when the
sodden ground slipped treacherously away beneath his
hooves. Despair beat against her more fiercely than the rain.
Her mind backtracked to the canyon. Had she done right to
leave? Maybe if she had stayed . . . *Esther, you could do
nothing. Now, stop thinking. You will surely go mad if you do
not. If you believe in the Lord, really believe you are going to
place this whole sorry mess in His hands. He is the only one
who can solve it.*

Strangely, the listless noncaring eased away and, when
dawn finally lightened the sky, Esther found herself straining
to see, straining until her eyes ached. What or who was she
looking for? Why did she think those two unreasonable men
would stop fighting and come looking for her? *Esther, stop!*

You promised yourself and the Lord not to consider that subject further.

Wrapped in the cold, sodden blanket and soaked to the skin, Esther began to shiver and her teeth started to chatter. The longer she rode, the more intensely she shook. Then, when the chills became almost unbearable, she began to grow drowsy. Her breathing became shallow and she felt light-headed. Swaying in the saddle, she caught herself just before she slid off. Finally the effort to ride was too much, and exhausted, she kicked free of the stirrups. Numb with cold, she hardly felt the jarring as she hit the ground.

Instinctively she curled into a ball and drifted away to a sandy bank by a gentle stream, a place where the sun shone hot and bright, warming her. She sighed with contentment and slept.

Savage let the tears course down his cheeks. In the dark and mixed with rain, Running Elk would never notice, so Savage made no effort to stem the flow. *Oh, God, let Esther be alive!* His mind cried words he had not thought to use in five years, years in which he had led a godless life. How dare he call on God now?

He looked helplessly across the rain-drenched plateau, the blackness shattered by the blue-white flashes of lightning, casting a brief, eerie, unholy glow over the bleak landscape. There was nowhere else to turn. He and Running Elk had ridden for miles, but the rain had washed away any trace of Esther's horse. The farther they rode, the more intense grew the foreboding that something had happened to her.

He felt and could almost see her hovering between life and death. If they delayed much longer, she would be dead.

Dawn brought with it no sun, only a half-lit world dissolved into distorted shapes by the ceaseless rain. A quick look at Running Elk showed his agony in the twisted features of his face. He was crying, too, and making no more effort to hide it than Savage.

The depth of despair that flooded Savage now was unlike any he had ever encountered. When he found his family dead, he felt guilt and grief, but there was nothing he could do to bring them back. This trek was different. Esther still lived . . . if they could but reach her in time.

"Running Elk, there has to be a clue," Savage signed, "something we're missing." He roared into the morning, giving vent to the anguish building in his heart. Then, before Running Elk could answer, they both spotted the mud-encrusted blanket hugging the ground.

The two men wheeled off their horses and crouched over the indistinct tracks of Esther's horse. In the rain-softened earth, the big stallion had left pock marks now filled with water. Leaping onto their horses, Savage and Running Elk hung out of their saddles, riding beside tracks that wandered aimlessly away from the blanket.

It was the better part of an hour before they saw the riderless horse standing in the distance, silhouetted against the dark sky. Though it went against every instinct, Savage kept reminding himself not to push his horse too hard in the unstable ground, and Running Elk took the same precaution. It would do Esther no good if they were injured and unable to reach her.

A soft, nervous nicker of welcome from Esther's horse was answered by the approaching ponies. It was not until they were nearly upon the pony that they saw an irregular heap on the ground, wrapped in a sodden, muddied blanket. The faithful animal was standing over Esther, making an effort to shield her body from the storm.

Both men leaped from their horses and raced to where Esther lay. "We've got to have a fire," Savage signed and shouted over the storm at Running Elk.

Running Elk nodded his understanding and Savage gave no more thought to him. *Dear Lord, do not let her be dead,* he pleaded as he stripped the blanket back. *Please do not let her be dead.*

His fingers felt her throat for a heartbeat and found a thin, reedy pulse. Her breath was irregular and shallow. "She's alive!" he shouted to Running Elk. Then, gently, Savage picked up the limp body.

"Bring her over here!" Running Elk answered back.

Savage slipped and slid his way toward a small shelter Running Elk had hastily constructed of oiled skins.

"I cannot make a fire in this rain," Running Elk moaned. "What do we do for warmth? She will die soon without it."

Savage stripped the wildcat skin from Esther's horse and shook off the water. He wrapped it around her, fur-side out. The shelter was not big enough to shelter them all, so the two men knelt in the pouring rain and massaged the circulation back into her legs and arms.

At last, the storm roared over and beyond them, leaving a clear blue sky in the west and the promise of sun in a little while. The quiet after the fury was strange and terrifying, for now they could hear the pauses growing longer between Esther's gasping breaths.

Savage felt again for her pulse and found it weaker. "She's dying," he sobbed and made no effort to disguise it. He picked up her slight body, feather-light in his arms, as if the spirit that gave it grace and strength had already fled beyond them. He clasped her to him, sobbing as he had never done, seeing the years without her stretch out like black beads on an endless chain. They had had so little time together, had never married and fulfilled their love, brought children into the world. They would never grow old together—

Then an unreasoning fury filled him. "Esther!" he shouted at the top of his voice. "If you die on me, so help me, I'll— I'll finish the fight with Running Elk, slice him to ribbons, hang his hair out to dry, and marry his Comanche princess. I swear I will, my beloved, I swear it!" The words issued forth in a babbling scream of rage, fear, and love so garbled they were barely understandable.

Esther, however, understood, for a ghost of a smile curved her still blue lips. Savage bent to hear her words, faint and slurred, "Then . . . you'd better . . . start collecting . . . horses—"

"Oh, God, thank you," he breathed. Cradling and rocking her slowly in his arms, he crooned to her as one would a baby until her breathing grew deeper, more regular and her pulsebeat stronger. Then, gently, he laid her down.

Savage felt Running Elk's eyes on them, heard the splashing in the puddles as the rain-soaked warrior came leading his horse up to the shelter. "It is time I go," he signed. "The Golden One has made her choice. Sometimes what is too near is not easily seen. The beautiful, loyal Star Flower waits for me, has always waited. I will go to her."

"You are a brave and wise man," Savage signed. "We will not fight again."

"I wish that were so, but with you leading the Army to the Comanche, we will meet as enemies. The next time there will be no Golden One to bring sense to our heads. We will kill each other, for I will never stop again until you are dead."

Savage eyed him through slitted eyes. Running Elk was

right. If they ever met again, with Savage as an army scout, it would be a duel to the death. "You have nothing to fear from me, my brother. I will not lead the Army to you and your people. I will not lead the Army again, ever. I am taking Esther away from here to a place that will make her very happy."

Running Elk looked down into Esther's bloodless face. "If you can hear me, my Golden One, know that if you are ever in need I will know and I will come to you." He leveled a stunning look at Savage. "If you do not make her happy . . . I will meet you sometime, somewhere, and you will pay."

The chief extended his hand. Savage grasped his wrist, and the two men welded a bond between brothers.

Then, like a graceful shadow, Running Elk sprang on his pony and was gone, the receding thuds of Raven's hooves sounding a melancholy tattoo over the deserted hills.

seventeen

Staring back from the borrowed mirror was a stranger. She was dressed in white ruffles and a flowing veil, her ivory hair curled in ringlets and held at the sides with fashionable combs. But something was wrong.

Tears welled in the azure eyes. *This isn't me*! Esther wanted to shout, *I can't get married looking like this*! But seeing the glowing faces of the delighted women of the wagon train, she could not bring the words to her lips.

Riding northwest, she and Savage had found a late train along the Oregon Trail, as he had predicted they would. And traveling with the wagon train was a preacher, also predicted. What was not as easily foretold, however, was the enthusiasm with which the weary travelers had halted in their journey to help the young couple tie the knot. Eager for something to celebrate, the pioneers had circled their wagons and pooled their finery to make this a memorable wedding day for Esther and Savage.

Dear Lord, what am I to do? she moaned silently, regarding her reflection with anguish.

As if in answer to her prayer, a small girl stepped forward shyly and handed her a bouquet of prairie grasses and weeds, tastefully arranged inside a ring of evergreen sprigs. Following behind the child was the young mother, her eyes wide with worry.

"I'm Anne Conklin," she said, introducing herself. "I'm so sorry, but this is the best we could do. We could not find a flower blooming anywhere." Her eyes flew around the

179

tent as she stiffened her back, bracing herself for the condemnation of the other women.

Before anyone could speak, however, Esther said, "This is a lovely bridal bouquet! I'm delighted. Thank you."

Anne and her daughter exchanged grateful smiles.

"Well, it certainly doesn't go with the rest of her lovely things," said the matriarch of the group, with an irritable snort.

"I have a solution for that," Esther put in. "Since there are no flowers to be had, I have something that will fit the bouquet."

Quickly, she removed the veil, stepped out of the layers of clothing, and ended with the removal of the high-heeled, pointed-toed shoes. With the shedding of each layer, the women's faces dropped a little until, by the time she had stripped away the last petticoat and stood in the fine muslin undergarments, they all looked thoroughly miserable.

"I know you think me ungrateful, but I am not used to such finery. I will be much more comfortable in my own clothes. In my pack there is a dress I think will be suitable."

Before Esther could say more, Anne dashed from the tent. An uneasy silence hovered over the proceedings as everyone waited for her to return. Within minutes, she came lugging the heavy pack. "Is this what you wanted?"

"It is. Thank you, Anne."

Esther handed the bouquet to the child for safekeeping, reached into the leather pouch, and brought out a carefully wrapped garment. She slipped the dress over her head. Makes Medicine had made the doeskin soft by tanning and chewing it for hours, then smoking it until it was as dainty as linen, as soft as velvet, and the palest of yellows, like rich, frothy cream. Thick fringe hung from the neckline and shoulders, brushing against her legs at the hemline that dipped long on the sides, and scalloped up over her knees in front and back. Dozens of small, metal cones fastened in clusters at the side seams and yoke, tinkled when she moved.

Anne then handed Esther a pair of thigh-high fringed leggings, painted a soft blue, beaded and belled. She tied the tops of the leggings to her breechclout. Beaded garters, worn just below the knee, held the leggings firmly in place. Finally came the high-topped moccasins—soft, fringed at the calves, and running down the single back seam.

Esther stepped away from the mirror, and the heavy fringe swayed as she moved, accentuating her long legs.

"You intend to wear *that* heathen thing to be married in?" The matriarch quirked her right eyebrow and sniffed her displeasure into a linen handkerchief.

Esther smiled gently. "I do believe it suits the bouquet, do not you?"

Removing the combs from her hair, she allowed the white-gold mass to tumble over her shoulders and down her back in a lush mane, shiny as an iridescent pearl.

When she turned, a quick intake of breath from the onlookers told Esther all she needed to know. Retrieving her bouquet, she announced in a soft, but determined voice, "I think I am ready."

"For a scalping party, not a wedding!" the matriarch huffed under her breath.

"Effie, do be quiet," Anne said crisply. "It isn't *your*

wedding. Besides, Esther looks as lovely as any bride I've ever seen and lovelier than most."

Anne held the flap of the tent open and the women, murmuring their good wishes, filed out. Another glance in the mirror, and Esther, too, stepped into the sun shining from a pale blue sky dimmed by thin high clouds. A cool breeze blew wisps of hair around her face as she walked toward the gathering crowd.

She gave the people and the nervous preacher only a cursory glance, for awaiting her arrival was Savage, looking more magnificent than she had ever seen him. Standing proud as the pines surrounding them, he wore a long leather hunting shirt scraped thin and dyed a pale cream color over dark blue leggings. His hair, shining in grizzled splendor, had been neatly trimmed, and a band of leather strung through beaten silver disks held it in place.

A look of delight swept over his face when he saw Esther, and his mouth tilted in a welcoming smile. Thick clusters of tiny metal cones sewn into the long fringes of his leggings jingled softly in rhythm to his moccasined steps as he walked to meet her. Somehow the sound was intensely masculine to Esther, and it stirred a warm, safe feeling deep inside.

Savage held out his hand, and Esther placed her own in his open palm and watched as the long sinewy fingers closed over it. With slow steps, he guided her to a position in front of the preacher, who was flipping nervously through a large worn Bible.

Having found what he was looking for, the preacher began reading, but Esther heard little he said. In awe, she studied Savage's classic profile silhouetted against the sky, the morning sun bronzing his strong face. His expression was that of a man at peace with himself and his God.

Oh, thank You, Lord, for giving me this man, Esther prayed. *With him beside me, I can walk tall and free, with my face to the sun. I can meet life with faith and hope and hear Your whispers on the wind, for I will no longer walk alone.*

Turning his head toward her, Savage looked deep into her eyes, now shimmering with tears, and sent a prayer heavenward. *Thank You, Father, for taking back a trail-hardened old sinner like me and giving me an angel like this woman. . . . It's hard to believe You could forgive me for all my black thoughts and deeds. But you've taken away the hatred and filled my heart with love. Now my life . . . our lives . . . are Yours.*

"And do you, Brook Savage, take this woman to be your lawfully wedded wife?" the preacher prompted.

With his eyes on Esther, Savage spoke. "Yes," he said, his voice husky with emotion.

"Then keep the commandments, children, and live with the Lord. You are now husband and wife." The deep booming voice of the preacher rolled over the hills, and the gathered witnesses let out a great cheer.

Underneath it all, however, Esther heard soft stirrings. All nature, which had appeared to be holding its breath until the sacred pronouncement, now erupted in a veritable cacophony of sound and motion. The playful breeze picked up, sighing through the evergreens. Crickets and other tiny woodland creatures chirped their delight. And eagles circled and plunged to earth in a breathtaking spectacle of flight.

At day's end, when they had ridden many miles along

the trail into their future, and Esther sank, exhausted, into the sweet, soft boughs Savage had gathered for their bed, she held out her hand and bade him come near. "It is the Indian way . . . wherever we are together, it is home."

In the golden glow of autumn, they rode at a leisurely pace for the better part of two weeks. Despite Esther's entreaties, however, Savage had not told her their destination.

"Won't you say where we are going?" she would ask. "I would like to know something of my future."

"You will know in good time" was his only reply as silver glints lit the gray of his eyes.

This afternoon on the Great Plain, with no shelter in sight, the sky was growing steadily darker, filling with great thunderheads that threatened a downpour at any minute. A chill breeze brought the scent of rain from the north, and the first crack of thunder sent Esther's horse skittering sideways in small leaps of panic.

Quickly, with quiet voice and firm hands on the reins, she brought the mare under control, but not before looking up to see a worried frown creasing Savage's face. "If you look like that every time I trip or my horse misbehaves," she teased, "you will be an old man before your time."

Though Savage gave a thin smile, the worry did not leave his face. He had not felt this tremendous weight of protective responsibility with his first family, and he could not help feeling that if he had, they might be alive today. Though it was foolish thinking, it weighed on him.

When the skies opened and the rain began, Esther turned up her face to catch the first drops. "I love rain," she said softly. "It was the rain that brought you to me."

She laughed gaily, and it was impossible to resist her mood though they were soon drenched.

When the misty shroud lifted for an instant, it was Esther who caught sight of the cabin. "Look, Savage! Surely whoever lives there will shelter us for the night."

The rain poured down again, blotting out the landscape, but they rode toward the spot where they had seen the building nestled in a grove of bare-branched trees. Savage seemed to be leaning forward in his saddle as though anticipating something.

"Is there danger?" she asked uncertainly.

"I do not think so."

Nevertheless, his body went rigid, and Esther swallowed against the fear that rose and tightened her throat.

Behind them an unexpected break in the clouds sent a shaft of sun through the gathering darkness. It spotlighted the meadow and created a brilliant sweeping rainbow that seemed to end at the front door of the small, tidy cabin. Esther gasped, speechless at the sight.

Pulling the horses to a stop at the front door, Savage motioned her forward. "I'll take care of the ponies. Why do not you knock and see if they will take us in?"

Since strong healthy men did not normally send their women to a stranger's door, Esther's eyes darted quickly to his face, but nothing in is expression suggested that anything was amiss. She opened her mouth to protest, then decided he must have a good reason for the unusual suggestion and clamped her lips shut.

Sliding off the sturdy mare, Esther sloshed her way to the weathered slab door. Before she could raise her hand to knock, however, the door opened wide and Esther found herself looking down into the face of a tiny birdlike woman.

The woman's once raven-black hair, streaked with silver-white, was pulled back from the translucent skin of a scarcely wrinkled forehead and held with a red scarf. One-half the woman's face was a vision of delicate beauty, but a rough disfiguring scar marred the other half.

Esther felt the strength drain from her body and she went numb. Whirling, she looked at Savage who stood at a distance, holding the reins of their horses and grinning widely. So he had known all along and had planned this as a wedding present!

Delirious with joy, she clasped the little woman in her arms and sobbed, "Aunt Mercy! Oh, Aunt Mercy!"

Esther had come home.

A Letter To Our Readers

Dear Reader:

In order that we might better contribute to your reading enjoyment, we would appreciate your taking a few minutes to respond to the following questions and return to:

Karen Carroll, Editor
Heartsong Presents
P.O. Box 719
Uhrichsville, Ohio 44683

1. Did you enjoy reading *Whispers on the Wind*?
   ❑ Very much. I would like to see more books by this author!
   ❑ Moderately
   ❑ I would have enjoyed it more if

   _____

2. Where did you purchase this book?_____

   _____

3. What influenced your decision to purchase this book?
   ❑ Cover   ❑ Back cover copy
   ❑ Title   ❑ Friends
   ❑ Publicity   ❑ Other _____

4. Please rate the following elements from 1 (poor) to 10 (superior).
   ❑ Heroine ❑ Plot
   ❑ Hero ❑ Inspirational theme
   ❑ Setting ❑ Secondary characters

5. What settings would you like to see in Heartsong Presents Books?

   _____

   _____

6. What are some inspirational themes you would like to see treated in future books?

   _____

   _____

7. Would you be interested in reading other Heartsong Presents Books?
   ❑ Very interested
   ❑ Moderately interested
   ❑ Not interested

8. Please indicate your age range:
   ❑ Under 18 ❑ 25-34 ❑ 46-55
   ❑ 18-24 ❑ 35-45 ❑ Over 55

Name _____

Occupation _____

Address _____

City_____ State _____ Zip _____

HAVE YOU MISSED ANY OF THESE TITLES?

These additional titles in our Romance Reader series contain two complete romance novels for the price of one. You'll enjoy hours of great inspirational reading. Published at $7.95 each, these titles are available through Heartsong Presents for $3.97 each.

_____ RR2 A MIGHTY FLAME &
   A CHANGE OF HEART *by Irene Brand*

_____ RR3 LEXI'S NATURE &
   TORI'S MASQUERADE *by Eileen M. Berger*

_____ RR5 SONG OF JOY &
   ECHOES OF LOVE *by Elaine Schulte*

_____ RR7 FOR LOVE ALONE &
   LOVE'S SWEET PROMISE *by Susan Feldhake*

_____ RR9 SUMMER'S WIND BLOWING &
   SPRING WATERS RUSHING *by Susannah Hayden*

_____ RR10 SECOND SPRING &
   THE KISS GOODBYE *by Sally Laity*

Send to: Heartsong Presents Reader's Service
P.O. Box 719
Uhrichsville, Ohio 44683

Please send me the items checked above. I am enclosing $_____ (please add $1.00 to cover postage and handling). Send check or money order, no cash or C.O.D.s, please.
To place a credit card order, call 1-800-847-8270.

NAME _____

ADDRESS _____

CITY / STATE _____ ZIP _____
RR

Great New Inspirational Fiction

from HEARTS♥NG PRESENTS

Biblical Novel Collection #1
by Lee Webber
Two complete inspirational novels in one volume.

_____ BNC1 **CALL ME SARAH**—Can Sarah, like Queen Esther
be used by God . . . even as a slave in Herod's place?
CAPERNAUM CENTURION—One Centurion's
life is irrevocably changed by his encounter with a
certain Nazarene.

Citrus County Mystery
Collection #1

by Mary Carpenter Reid
Two complete inspirational mystery and romance novels in one volume.

_____ CCM1 **TOPATOPA**—Can Alyson Kendricks make an historic
village come alive . . . without becoming history herself?
DRESSED FOR DANGER—Roxanne Shelton's
fashion designs were the key to her success . . . but
did they unlock a closet of secrets?

*BOTH COLLECTIONS ARE AVAILABLE FOR $3.97 EACH THROUGH
HEARTSONG PRESENTS. ORIGINALLY PUBLISHED AT $7.95 EACH.*

Send to: Heartsong Presents Reader's Service
P.O. Box 719
Uhrichsville, Ohio 44683

Please send me the items checked above. I am enclosing
$_____(please add $1.00 to cover postage and handling).
Send check or money order, no cash or C.O.D.s, please.
To place a credit card order, call 1-800-847-8270.

NAME _____

ADDRESS _____

CITY / STATE _____ ZIP_____
BNC1/CCMC1

LOVE A GREAT LOVE STORY?

Introducing Heartsong Presents —
Your Inspirational Book Club

Heartsong Presents Christian romance reader's service will provide you with four never before published romance titles each month! In fact, your books will be mailed to you at the same time advance copies are sent to book reviewers. You'll preview each of these new and unabridged books before they are released to the general public.

These books are filled with the kind of stories you have been longing for—stories of courtship, chivalry, honor, and virtue. Strong characters and riveting plot lines will make you want to read on and on. Romance is not dead, and each of these romantic tales will remind you that Christian faith is still the vital ingredient in an intimate relationship filled with true love and honest devotion.

Sign up today to receive your first set. Send no money now. We'll bill you only $9.97 post-paid with your shipment. Then every month you'll automatically receive the latest four "hot off the press" titles for the same low post-paid price of $9.97. That's a savings of 50% off the $4.95 cover price. When you consider the exaggerated shipping charges of other book clubs, your savings are even greater!

THERE IS NO RISK—you may cancel at any time without obligation. And if you aren't completely satisfied with any selection, return it for an immediate refund.

TO JOIN, just complete the coupon below, mail it today, and get ready for hours of wholesome entertainment every month.

Now you can curl up, relax, and enjoy some great reading full of the warmhearted spirit of romance.